I0525155

Modest Aspirations

Poems by
Gerald Locklin

Stories by
Beth Wilson

LUMMOX Press

©2010 by Gerald Locklin (poems) & Beth Wilson (stories)

All Rights Reserved. No portion of this book may be reproduced without express written permission of the authors, except for purposes of review.

ISBN 978-1-929878-08-6

First edition

Lummox Press
PO Box 5301
San Pedro, CA 90733
www.lummoxpress.com

Printed in the United States of America

Acknowledgements:
Good in Bed and *Vanessa Bell: Charleston Gardens, 1933* first appeared in The New York Quarterly; other poems first appeared in Ambit (London); Askew; Big Hammer; Chiron Review; Coagula Art Journal; Fight These Bastards; 5 AM; Freefall; Genre; Iconoclast; King's Estate Press; La Nouvelle Revue Moderne (Paris); Minotaur; Nerve Cowboy; Pearl; Presa; Quercus Review; Silt Reader; Slipstream; Southern California Review (USC); and Tears in the Fence (Dorset).

Dedications

To RD Armstrong, Beth Wilson,
Eileen Klink, and all my loyal editors
and publishers who selflessly do
so much for so many.

—Gerald Locklin—

Thanks to Gerry, RD, Chris,
and everyone else who had a part in
getting my work out there so people
can see it. And thanks to Ken
for taking care of everything so I
would have time to write.

—Beth Wilson—

Table of Contents

PERSONAL LOANS:

Introduction

My relationship with Gerald Locklin has been somewhat colorful...Over the past fifteen years or so our paths have repeatedly crossed as various projects have come and gone. Even though I was never one of his students (at least not an *enrolled* one), through him I have met and published a number of talented writers and poets. And I have also had the pleasure of publishing him in both the Lummox Journal (a magazine that I put out monthly for nearly eleven years) and the Little Red Book series (a chapbook series that I'm still doing).

I could wax poetic here and say what a great guy he is and how supportive and encouraging he has been over the years, but what really matters is that Gerry continues to produce well-crafted poetry. Ultimately, that is what matters. I think this collection demonstrates that. Plus, as readers, we get to meet yet another member of his expanding posse, Beth Wilson, whose short stories are wonderful in their own right.

So, I hope you enjoy these poems and stories, as you are reading some of the best danged writing around!

RD Armstrong
Publisher
Lummox Press

NEW POEMS

Gerald Locklin

GOOD IN BED

I don't understand why guys worry about
Whether they are ranked good or bad in bed
By the ladies who presume to
Adjudicate such performances.
After all the very fact that they're talking about you
Indicates something is commanding their sexual interest.
Furthermore, if any woman ever claimed
That *I* were less than excellent in bed,
I'd know that it must be *her fault,*
Not only because,
As the terpsichorean proverb observes,
It takes a minimum of two to tango,
But, definitively, because I can testify
From personal experience,
That I have always been
Sensational even when in bed
Only with myself.

WIFE OF EASTER BUNNY

One of Toad's buddies at the pool
Says, "I hate religion; I hate all
Religions. When I think religion,
I think war, famine, pestilence,
Persecution, sexual repression,
Violent sublimations...just about
Everything bad in the history of
The world..."

"...and furthermore," he says,
"there's no more empirical evidence
For belief in a deity than for the
Tooth-fairy or Santa Claus. You might
As well be worshipping the Easter Bunny!"

"Wait a minute," Toad says;
"You're trying to tell me
The Easter Bunny isn't real?
Then who the fuck hides
The raw eggs in my shoes?"

VANESSA BELL: *charleston garden, 1933*

the woman garbed in rose
sews a lily garment
draped across her lap.
the sun breaks through the ample foliage
that lines the pathway to the formless door.
even the impressionistic sky/sea upholstery
of the chair the woman sits on
is a work of art.
everything about the place is.
vanessa, clive, and duncan
excelled in the decorative,
the arts of civilized living,
the apotheosis of the unnecessary.
in england and wales, i battled pulmonary
emboli from heathrow back to heathrow.
my son and I killed time in the garden,
while my wife and daughter viewed the
artifacts inside the cottage. We yawned and
sweated and rehydrated. i remember
the long lane on and off the property.

i battled my wife too, but (sorry, ladies)
didn't batter her. i could barely make it up
the hills and endless staircases. temporarily
the exercise helped, though. the spirits and
the ales helped even more.

within six weeks i'd be in intensive care in
california, my drinking days already melting
to nostalgia, then indifference.

my wife would love to be the woman in this
painting, with her life of art and crafts and
living but inhuman things.

she's read a tower of books about
bloomsbury, and remembers them, she can
even keep straight their genealogy of morals,
the entanglements, arrangements, and paternities,
that always fail me in my literature classes,
as futile as teaching *lie* and *lay.*

i'll never be able to give her charleston farm.
not to mention sissinghurst or knole, but
she's turned our modest home into a poor-man's
(woman's) monk's house, and made me assent
to the possibility of a return,
five years from now, when she retires,
to england and to wales (where i taught a term
in 1989: we lived in menai bridge and gazed
across the straights at bangor and snowdonia).
i'm not sure what her feelings are towards
the more virile ireland and scotland.

And i'm afraid i may be fool enough to do it.

A Blossoming

On Easter Sunday morning
On my Sirius car radio
I heard a saxophonist playing "Blossom,"
And I knew that Sonny Rollins
Had to be the man, No one else
Pours every breath of every extended riff
Of every dance of every strophe into
The molecular complexity of life itself,
Including its response to the antistrophe
Of death. Losing ourselves in such resurrection-requiems,
We know that death does not succeed in cheating
Us of life, that Blake and Rollins-all of the anointed-
Intuited that Eternity and every Instant are inseparable.
Time is the greatest lie,
And Loss the worst illusion:
The grave, the funeral pyre, decomposition:
All are movements of a single symphony.
Someone strode out of that sepulcher.
He was smiling and his wounds were healed.
He was singing and he even felt that he might be allowed
A little swagger. There was laughter in his leap.

The longer Sonny lives, the more of us he lives on in,
And the more he sounds like the sun.

MY FINEST MOMENT

Gerald Locklin/New Poems

I'm shopping at my youngest daughter's
Favorite jewelry store- Luna, in Belmont Shore-
For her 30th birthday, a little something extra,
A "daddy-gift" in addition to what my wife
And I will splurge on together.
I'm attired as usual like a homeless guy.
In front of the display case, a chic salesgirl joins me:
"What is your price range, Sir?"

And for once in my life, just this once in my life,
I allow myself the arrogance of answering, quietly,
"I don't see anything that's not within it."

And when she finally finds me something
Not entirely unworthy of my beautiful, beloved child,
I purchase it without inquiring the price,
Or glancing at the tag.

ADVANCE MEDICAL DIRECTIVE

If I should ever collapse in public,
My fervent wish is that Mouth-to-Mouth
Resuscitation be administered only by
The most beautiful woman (or women)
In the vicinity.

The activity should continue
For at least an hour after the last vital sign
Has seemingly expired.

Even at that point,
All hope should not be abandoned there,
But the strategy should be shifted
From Mouth-to-Mouth to Mouth-to Dick.

Come to think of it,
In the spirit of Preventative Medicine,
Why don't we just get started
Right now?

Wynton Marsalis and the Jazz at Lincoln Center Orchestra

Gerald Locklin/New Poems

He is no longer boyish of face or physique.
But he is more relaxed, witty and modest,
Almost self-deprecating,
Confident in the commanding success he has achieved
As a musician, composer, conductor, arranger,
Educator, administrator, and dark eminence behind
The Ken Burns PBS Jazz Documentary Series
With its focus upon the white man's appropriation
Of the Black Man's (and woman's) Music.
(Well, we certainly loved it, learned from it,
Played it, profited from it-sorry, Wynton- and
Today are largely responsible for preserving it.)

He's lost his brashness and gained maturity,
Equanimity, even as he has retained and smoothed
His skill, his chops, and his vast knowledge of
The History of Music, of All the Musics. He is
A walking, talking Encyclopedia of World Music
(Of the Musics of the World) and can demonstrate
The undeniable interactions that have flowed into
The Present: His and The Orchestra's, for instance.

And yet what was missing at the beginning,
And none of us, black or white, could really
Help but notice it, is still not there:
The *je-ne-sais-quoi*, the ineffable, the inexplicable,
The difference between the Poet Made and the Poet Born,
What Billie and Louis and Frank and Pablo
And Miles and Trane and even (maybe) Chet Baker had:
That thing we still call Soul.

God, Evolution, History, Life,
Whatever you want to call the Creator, the Causality,
The Committee of Causes,
Is not an Equal Opportunity Provider,

Some are given more than others.
No one is given nothing.
But no one is given everything either.
The more you are given, the more likely it is

That something essential will be withheld.
Wynton Marsalis was given (and strove for)
Everything except the ultimate ingredient
Of Immortality. I guess it went elsewhere.

He seems reconciled to that,
And he's a brilliant, good, and generous human being.
He seems to be having fun.

Life is not fair: that's why we crave an Afterlife.
But Life does have its own genius in compensations:
Consider the life of John Keats
(Excuse his color, please):
Its brevity. Its endlessness

Boucher: *Venus and Mercury Instructing Cupid, 1738*

What they seem to be instructing him in
Are the secondary erogenous zones,
In this case a spot in the soft flesh
Of the inner forearm just above the pearl bracelet.
I assume they will move upward and around
To the even softer flesh of the upper arm,
The upper thigh, the neck and earlobe,
Kisses not quite on the mouth,
The individual attention to the toes,
The teasing to erection of the nipples,
Tickling of the anus.
And if she has a belly,
Rather than pretending to ignore it,
I hope they will clutch it, knead it, sink their faces
Into it, beg it, privilege it, tug her golden locks
Back to the nape of her neck, massage her eyes,
Her temples, inflame her flesh, from follicles to
The soles of her feet, Make her cry out
To be taken.

Boucher: *Venus Disarming Cupid, 1751*

This Cupid is one ugly runt.
There's no way that his pygmy wings
Could elevate his early-onset chub-besity.
My wife suggests his bloody buttocks
Might be caused by diaper rash.
The face of an angel?
More that of a pugilist.
In general, his epidermis has been
Tinted with and tainted by
The most hideous red on the palette.

In contrast (deliberately?) this is perhaps
The most lovely of the Venuses.
If indeed it is Madame de Pompadour,
Only recently furloughed as consort of Louis XV,
Then it is indeed a good thing to be king,
And the artist does indeed enhance her re-invention
As a Vestal Virgin. Her tiny nipples, on barely discernible
Areolae, are the pale pink of her lips and even paler cheeks.
(I bet her labia are too.) Her limbs are of flesh, but
Minimally muscled: No royal health-club regimen
For her century of courtesans. A slender thumb and
Forefinger have turned the point of the dart
Back at Cupid. The gentlest breeze softens her curls.
She is bemused by carnal love and has survived it,
Unscathed, unscarred, indelibly untouched…
And in no need of tattoos, J.-Patrice Marandel
Credits "her success with the king" to "Fidelity and
Discretion." I'd guess a little of both would go a long
Way in our own time. A white dove at her foot

Reclines subserviently beneath the beak of her mate.
And yet who truly ruled the roost?

The benevolence of her smile,
The empyrean blue of the white goddess,
The embrace of her powerful thighs,
A string of precious pearls as pledge of exclusivity-
Who would not abandon all to be disarmed by
Her submission, vanquished by the conquest of
The most intimate beauty ever consecrated.

Boucher: *Cupid Wounding Psyche,* 1741

She never thought she needed it,
Was satisfied with thought
And the inverse superiority of purity,
Self-discipline, denial, The Higher Nature, Spirit,
Soul, a cryogenics of the physical.
He'll show her what she has been missing.
Even as the arrow approaches penetration,
She's already leaning back,
Learning to uncross her ankles,
Her hand grown bold between his legs,
Her lips about to part,
Her gaze about to roll back
In intoxication.
The sacred psalms made wet
With the hormonal juices,
She's about to be initiated into the
Purgatorial Pilgrimage towards Hellfire
Or Paradise.

Josh Nelson, Jazz Pianist

A friend of mine, Joanne France,
Who is an avid supporter of the arts,
Has been touting for the last few years
A young jazz pianist, Josh Nelson,
A graduate of Long Beach State's music program,
Who studied under Buddy Collette and Cecilia Coleman
Before moving on to Boston's famed
Berklee College of Music. Each month she would forward
His email newsletter of upcoming appearances,
So one warm summer Sunday evening,
I hopped in my Ford Focus and drove up
To hear him at the Jazz Bakery.

The crowd was small,
Mostly his loyal young followers,
And one old guy, me, sitting alone
A few rows back on the aisle.
He was a little nervous at first,
As well he should have been,

The bakery is big-time, a comfortable auditorium
Where I've heard the likes of Art Farmer, Roy Hargrove,
Ahmad Jamal, Toshiko Akiyoshi, McCoy Tyner,
Nneena Freelon, Cedar Walton, Cyrus Chestnut, Benny Golson,
Terrence Blanchard, Pharaoh Sanders, and Harold Land,
Just to sample the roster. But then he lay his fingers
On the keys and from the first arpeggio
We were dealing with a world-class talent,
As composer, arranger, theoretician, and certainly
Performer—maybe not yet as lyricist: Leave the poetry
To me, kid, or at least take a Directed Studies from me!

He reminded me most of some of the great Scandinavian
Musicians whose work I've been sent by Henry Denander:
E.S.T., Alfred Ayler, Tord Gustavson, Bobo Stenson,
Anders Jormin, Lars Gullin, Paul Bley, Harald Johnsen,
Jarle Vespestad ... with a touch on the periphery

Of John Surman, Dave Douglas, and Keith Jarrett.
Maybe the local film greats, Alan Broadbent and Bill Cunliffe.
Of course, he was reared on Joni Mitchell and James Taylor—
Not my crowd—a little on the soft-boiled side—but I can't expect
Frank Sinatra , Judy Garland, Nat King Cole, to mean the same
To his generation as to mine. He'll gradually come to embrace
Them all, and he already knows his classics and his avant-garde.

What it comes down to is that he has prepared himself
In every way for greatness. He's served multiple
Apprenticeships, as Dave and Phil Alvin did with the blues.
He knows where he's coming from, and the excitement
Of where he's heading has begun.

On his first CD, *Let It Go,* he's joined by Seamus Blake,
Anthony Wilson, Matt Wilson, Derek Oleszkiewicz,
Sara Gazarek, and the Supernova String Quartet.
Mark Weber once asked me on the radio
Why I go to hear jazz live. These are my reasons:

The first is the essential, intrinsic human pleasure
(And consolation) of music in any context. Another is to be taken
Inside and outside of myself. Thirdly, music is the
Anti-toxic intoxication. But there is also this:
The thrill of watching as A Star is Born,
A kind of aesthetic Nativity Scene.
Who would have wanted
To have been late for the First One?

The Death of Norman Mailer
(For Gene Dinielli)

Reading his obit in the *New York Times,*
And, how, in his final years,
Even Gore Vidal stayed over at his place,
To reminisce about old battles,

I find that I am near to tears.

And when, later, someone says,
"But he never did write
The Great American Novel,"

I say, "No, he only managed to record
The most vital first-hand testimony
To the second half of the 20th Century,

Not to mention being, with Truman Capote, Hunter
Thompson, and Tom Wolfe, a pillar of a new genre,
The Non-Fiction Novel, and of the New (or Gonzo)
Journalism, which all burgeoned into the adding
Of Creative Non-Fiction to university curriculums,

And, by the way, you may want to give a gander
To *The Deer Park* and *The Naked and the Dead* sometime:
But not before you embark on your own first novel...
Because you might find yourself not up to the competition,

And competition is something Norman Mailer
"Did Not Fear."

Then I turn away before I can give in to my inclination
To take a swing at him (something Mailer might have
Done but probably wouldn't have), just to let him
Know that literary testosterone, though diminished by
The death of Norman Mailer, did not go up in smoke
Completely with his sacred ashes.

Alfred Steiglitz: *A Portrait: Georgia O'Keeffe, 1918*, photograph

This portrait is of her right hand alone,
As it clutches, between two buttons,
A sweater or jacket.

Her face is not shown.
Nothing of her is in the photo except
Her hand and her garment.

The catalogue explains that he took
Hundreds of photos of her,
Which he called a "portrait in time,"
And that he felt it sometimes required
This multiplicity of images
"To capture the complexity
Of a human personality."

I agree.
That's why I write so many poems.
And sometimes early poems will get
Hurled back in my face
As evidence of a seeming inconsistency
Or hypocrisy.

But why should a sixty-seven-year-old man
Be consistent with his twenty-five-year-old
Self? Why should this morning's voice
Be the same as last evening's? Why should we
Assume the younger man was wiser?

Are your emotions, anxieties, enthusiasms,
The same upon arising as they were at bedtime?
Do you never debate issues within yourself?
Should a writer never give voice to
Conflicting points of view?

The Canker in the Rose

How the photographers, artists, poets
Of the first two hundred years
Loved our republic,
Celebrated it,
Iconized its bridges
To and beyond its borders,
In and out of the American consciousness,
To the Infinite:
Stella, Bourke-White, Crane...
Now, since World War Two,
We have determinedly defeated ourselves,
Defaced ourselves,
Addicted ourselves to chemicals, ease,
Illusions, rationalizations, Irony
(The Ironic Fist in the Velveteen Glove?).
We will die for nothing, and thus
We have rendered our deaths meaningless.
Is it any wonder that our art of the postmodern
Dwells only in the past,
Feeds on the onion skins
Of its Dead Fathers?
Only our immigrants appreciate America,
Though some forget or are taught
To rail against the obstacles
They knew awaited them.
Ah well, 'twas ever thus,
In Athens, Rome, Gay Paree,
Stiffnecked London and Berlin,
Weary Moscow—and, after our fall,
The rise and fall of Beijing and Tehran
Will be mercurial.

Jasper Johns: *Ale Cans*, 1964

They are not beer cans;
They are cans of Ballantine's (Pale) Ale,
The finest mass-produced American example
Of the master-brewer's art,
Testified to by Ernest Hemingway
And broadcast sponsor of the New York Yankees,
In the halcyon days of Mantle, Maris, Martin,
McDougal, Berra, Bauer, Whitey Ford,
Moose Skowron, and Elston Howard.
The bottle was famous for
Its Triple-X and Three-Ring Sign.

My friend and longtime officemate,
Chuck Stetler, described its taste as "skunky."
He was right, but unlike most New World beers and ales,
It at least *had* some taste,
Wasn't piss-water. It must have meant
Something to Jasper Johns; it meant a
Great deal—in both senses—to me: it meant
That it was worth its premium price.
And it meant the Age of Innocence,
And that, for me, it's never absolutely ended.

The Museum of Fine Arts, Boston

It does not own as many famous paintings
As the Art Institute of Chicago,
The Met, MOMA, the National Gallery, or even, perhaps,
The Los Angeles County Museum of Art,

But I'm impressed to find so many a-typical
Yet striking works by world-class artists.

Take "Carmeline," for instance:
Now this is not what springs to mind
When I think Henri Matisse:
No pastels, no window onto Nature,
No soft lines, gaiety, chinoiserie.

The woman's face is mannish,
And her flesh angry, defiant.
She holds a cloth against her cunt,
Almost stuffs it — in urban savagery — into herself.
The catalogue lies that the reds and blues
Are "vibrant," the earth tones "warm."
The former are, in fact, overwhelmed
By the latter, which are sepulchral.

Don't get me wrong:
I'm taken by this painting, intrigued.
It's like Gauguin repatriated to a
Bare-bones Paris. It's what Modigliani
Might have turned into, had he lived
Out of passion into disenchantment.
It's on the verge of Lucian Freud.
And yet this young Matisse grew into visual ecstasy.

Go figure.

I'm reminded of Bob Dylan's classic line,

with which in certain moods
I too identify:

"But I was so much older then;
I'm younger than that now."

(And a footnote to my students:
Please observe Bob's seven classic ballad iambs.)

Magritte: *Personal Values,* 1952

I do not value combs,
Nor am I intimidated by those
The size and toothiness of sharks.

Similarly, a clothes brush occupies no place
In or upon my closet of vanities.

I prefer the eternal verity of temporality.

A billowy pillow is, however,
All right with me.

An empty glass and a pencil without paper
Look too much like
The way my life's been going lately.

Centennial Ball, Metropolitan Museum, New York, 1969

Not a raving beauty, just
Unremarkably so, yet, in this photograph,
An eye-stopper.

The fatuous fellow in tux and bow-tie
Desires what she can give him,
But either won't or no longer wants to
Give her what she wants, and she's
No longer even sure what that is,
Except she knows it isn't him,
If, in fact, it ever was.
Passion, she deserves, but passion
Is so quickly quelled.

Is her Egyptian jewelry
That of Slave Girl or of Queen?
Is she too flat-chested,
Her arms too thin,
Her hair not long or short enough,
Her features or complexion
Just this evening passing slightly,
Past its prime?

Is she his wife or mistress?
Is he declining once again
To leave his wife, or is he
Calling his wife back from a brink?

In 1969 not even Dylan knew
The oxygen had gone out of
America.

On the Sublime and the Subliminal

Listening to Maurice Brown
On my car stereo
A couple of weeks ago,
I caught an unusual and enigmatic riff
That I vowed to go back and find
And listen to repeatedly,
To try to fathom it,
Its magic and its provenance.

I've returned a number of times now
But I haven't found it yet.
Unless it's vanished from my CD,
Maybe onto the classical FM station.
I guess it will show up again
Sometime when I'm least expecting it.

It's serendipitous moments like that
That the aesthete lives for,
The trickle of falling notes
At the climax of Miles Davis' "Solea,"
The Mona Lisa smile or that of
The Girl with Pearl Earring.

Perhaps a phrase of your own
That channeled itself through your pen
With a minimum of conscious mediation
Towards a poem or story
That never made it onto paper.

Or maybe a gasp-inducing touch
That occurs in lovemaking,
A spontaneous combustion.

The surrealists tried to find mechanisms
For releasing these mysterious slips
Of inspiration,

But they should have known
The unconscious will not be dictated to
By the technocratic ego.

As Keats knew,
You just have to keep on keeping on,
In a wise passivity
And allow the lost chords
To resurface, unbidden, unannounced
When you most need them.

A River Cruise, Calendar Photo, Getty Images

Five hundred children take the cruise
Beneath the tower drawbridge
From Westminster to Greenwich and back.
It's the one trip I urge every tourist to take,
Not to miss St. Paul's, Docklands, River Pubs,
The wharf where Bill Sykes met his end,
The Royal Naval College, the Observatory,
Zero Ground of Greenwich Mean Time,
The swirling tidal currents and the serpentine
Paths of the water thoroughfare itself,

The massive flood barrier just downstream.
The Thames is London, is its raison d'etre
(with due respect to Beefeaters and Tower Guards),
the bloodstream, sewer, wealth, and cemetery.
The Thames divides and bonds;
Pollutes and freshens.
To paraphrase John Irving,
Shit and hope both float.
The Thames is as enduring as the monarchy,
May prove more so.
The tribunes and the tributaries of the City flow to it;
The trains depart and barn there.
Even the Irish end up either here or there.
Europe cannot ignore it.
The colonies are colonizing it.
Even I, not understanding why,
Keep daring it to kill me.

All Things to All Men

She says, "I saw a bumper sticker yesterday
That said, 'God's last name is not DAMMIT!'"

Toad asks, "What is His last name,
FUCKIT?"

Georges Seurat: *Woman Strolling*

If you don't believe me,
Take another look
At what I will always call,
A la Sondheim,
"Sunday in the Park with Georges."

Seurat, like Bukowski,
Loved big butts.

The whole society did.

Centuries of society and art did.

Somewhere we went wrong.

But as I look around these days,
I conclude, "We'd better start learning
To like them again."

Vincent Van Gogh:
Postman Joseph Roulin, 1888

Can we ever look
too often
At a painting by Van
Gogh?

Perhaps, but not this one.

I read Van Gogh's description
of
"A man who is neither
embittered.
Nor sad, nor perfect, nor happy,
Nor always irreproachably
right...
But such a good soul and so
wise
And so full of feeling and so
truthful,"

And I hearken back to when,
A teenager, I read *Dear Theo,*
Vincent's letters to his brother,
And I see the words embodied in
The postman's face, beard, hands,
Blue uniform and cap, blue eyes, blue sky,
All Blues, No Blues, Eternal Verity of Blue,

And suddenly it strikes me
that,
My God!—Van Gogh was no less
Poet than he was a painter-
He even anticipated the
parataxic style
That Juan Gris and Picasso

Passed to Gertrude Stein,
From whom Ernest Hemingway
Adapted and perfected it.

I bet if you'd handed him
A saxophone, he would have
Metamorphosed into Coltrane,
Vanished into the exultative
choruses
Of A *Love Supreme.*

Vincent Van Gogh: *Entrance to the Public Gardens in Arles,* 1888

One by one the intermittent entrants
disappear into the garden.
The watchers in black on their park benches
Watch and only watch.
The sand has a different swirl from that of
The catalyzing officious sun.

The thick hick reads the daily news,
Which is never new:
That our dust is molecules,
And molecules to molecules
We shall return.

We emerge from the public garden
Of the molecules, and we return to it.

Colors are especially molecular,
As are brushstrokes.

This is, as Dylan Thomas also knew
The entrance/exit and the exit/entrance
Of the physical, the bodily, the earthen form,

And yet this garden tells us,
As its cultivator
In his "outcry of the soul"

That there must be something else as well.

Edward Weston's Martini Recipe

He painted his friend,
Imogen Cunningham.
Eventually he slept with her.

In 1923 he left his wife
and moved to Mexico
with Tina Modotri,
his model and lover.

Much earlier he had painted
and slept with his friend,
the photographer,
Margrethe Mather.
Cotton Mather might have
withheld approval,
but Edward certainly knew how
to choose his friends.

Sonya Noskowiak 'became his student,
assistant, model, and lover,'
according to a brochure.
(Right now I'd settle for a typist.)

I don't find the nudes of Charis Wilson
attractive: too abstract and too skinny.
But they obviously found each other
interesting, for over a decade.

I'm not criticizing.
I'm admiring his sense of pattern,
just as I'm amused by Cage and Glass.

I mean, This was a guy who really knew how
to mix business and pleasure.

Friday Night Lights

What a great life I've had—
Kids, literature, California—
And yet just like these young men
Trying to play their way out of
Odessa, Texas,

I am still at times afflicted by
The what-might-have-beens
If that pass had not glanced off my fingertips;
If I'd grown a few more inches;
Been a little faster, tougher, springier,
Braver, or more reckless;
If I could have actualized my daydreams.

My friends have often also been frustrated jocks:
D., the near-Olympic swimmer;
B., the near-Olympic Water Polo player;
D., the high school pitching phenom;
R., the running back turned aspiring actor...

In fact we all saw enough of the world
Of athletic success to know how lucky we are
To have flunked out of it,

But try telling that to the little boys
That you give birth to,
Or the little boy inside of you
Whose voice will never cease to narrate
The bittersweet scenarios of heroism.

Carpe Noctem

We are always being urged
By our parents and teachers
(Who don't really mean it)
To be less like sheep,
Not to follow the leader
But to think for ourselves.

I know what is meant by that,
But I've always cautioned my writing students
Not to think too much,
Which can be abstract and intimidating,
But to let their instincts and unconscious minds
And the emerging sounds of the words themselves
Write a lot of the poem for them,
Especially the first draft.

The great Portuguese poet,
Fernando Pessoa,
Went me one better, though:
In his *Keeper of Sheep* poems
He urges us not to think at all.
Like Gerard Manley Hopkins,
Who had been reading Duns Scotus,
Pessoa is a nominalist who puts his trust
Not in universals, but on the uniqueness
Of the individual, the particular,
The *quiddity* or *thisness*
Of the thing or person.
He instructs us to emulate the sheep and the flowers.

Come to think of it, Robinson Jeffers didn't prize
Very highly the adjectival part
Of the "rational animal" either.
Neither did Cummings, Bukowski, or Prévert.

All I know is that our cats seem to enjoy
A better quality and greater quantity of sleep

Than I do, especially around tax time:
In fact they sleep all night long
And most of the day,

Whereas I find that in order to fall back to sleep
I have to force myself to think mindless thoughts.

I've even been known to count sheep.

Personally I Always Insist on Speaking to George Washington

After she'd concluded the details of her financial
transaction,
My friend "J" asked the bank's phone representative
If he was allowed to tell her
Where he was located.

"Oh yes," he said, "I am in India."

"And yet you said your name was Abraham."

"Oh yes, we are encouraged to adopt
An American-sounding name."

"Do you have an American last name also?"

"Oh yes," he said, "it is *very* American—
I knew it would instill the greatest confidence in me:

It is Lincoln."

MORE UNSOLICITED ADVICE TO THE YOUNG

It is better to be a rich kid in Beverly Hills
Writing out of the abandoned heart
Of a rich kid in Beverly Hills, than a poor kid
In Watts or Ireland trying to write out
Of the monstrously humiliated heart of
Charles Bukowski, at the age of *25,* serving as
A "Go-Fer" in exchange for free drinks
In the boring and embattled bars of Philly.

And the closest thing to Another Bukowski
That I've come across in my recent reading
May well be his erstwhile mistress
And mother of his only child,
Frances (FrancEyE) Smith,
Who led the Counter-Life to his own,
And whose subjects, sympathies, and eccentricities
He could not embrace,
But who shared the plainspoken candidness
That characterized his own work at its best,
And who, like him, has lived to her final pallet
The life of the poet.

The Elizabethan sonneteer, Michael Drayton,
Instructed himself and us
To look in our hearts and write.

He said to look in ours,
Not *his* or *Charles Bukowski's.*

Robert Peake: *Portrait of a Woman, Possibly Frances Cotton of Broughton Castle, Northamptonshire, circa 1605*

Her fingers are too bony.
Her nose is too pointy.
Her hair (or wig) is too frizzy.
Her bib seems to choke her.
Her ornate gown seems to
Imprison her in armor.
Her jewelry seems to tell us,
"Noli me tangere,
For I am Caesar's."
But the twinkle in her eye,
And pursing of her small mouth
Seem to say, "Take the risk
And make me yours, and I will make it
Worth your while; I'll give you
The ride of a lifetime, one to savor
All the way to the gallows."

The Berlin Wall

I saw it in a magazine today,
An advertisement with a photo of Mikhail Gorbachev
Returning from a conference.
I don't even remember what the product was;
So much money gets wasted
On utterly useless ads and commercials.
I suppose in some way the expenditures
Benefit the economy.
But I was surprised once again
By how low the wall actually was.
I bet there were players in the NBA
Who could have leapt it.
But how few of the oppressed ever did manage
The escape to freedom?
It took us a quarter of a marriage
To erect our own Berlin Wall.
I always thought that one day
We would tear it down.
We never did. And now, two days before
The New Age of Hope, I know our Berlin Wall
Will withstand it.

Milton Avery

i know the modern artist says
it is his *choice* to draw
the human form this way,
These clunky, chunky rectilinear
ladies, for instance, that it is
impossible to imagine making love with,
even in the absence of
a viable same-species alternative.

i know they say they could as easily
have drawn with elegance and finesse,
with an eye and hand for representative details.

i know i'm watching realism
on its way into abstraction
or back into the primitive,
the tribal, archetypal.

and i do believe picasso
could have painted any way
he wanted to.
andy warhol too.

maybe milton avery.

but i bet a lot of guys
were just lunkheads,
like the early punk musicians
who, hamfisted, didn't have
to work at all to master
the expropriation of the
amateurish.

(A BUSY SUNDAY)

One sunny Sunday afternoon
Toad ends up swimming at the pool
with two women about whom
he has written stories which have,
as fate would have it, been published
in the same collection. Both are very
attractive. Neither is particularly attracted
to him, although both like him as a friend.

One knows he writes about her and loves it,
shows what he writes to her friends
and fellow office workers.

The other doesn't, and most likely never will.

Neither is a literary woman. He introduces them
to each other; some instinctive recognition
passes between them.

Toad basks in the beauty of his lily pond.

EDVARD MUNCH: SUMMER NIGHT'S DREAM (THE VOICE), *1893*

It's nice to see a voice
That isn't screaming for a change.
It's nice to see a virgin maiden
Leaning towards me,
Even if she's also innocently hesitant,
Even if her offering
Is painfully belated.

It's nice to think of Bergman's
Smiles of a Summer Night,
A-typical and yet perhaps that perfect note
Of bittersweet and melancholy,
Reconciliation, absolution,
Dying wisdom and the springing hope
Of youthful lovers.

It's nice to listen to
A Little Night Music,
Both Bach and Sondheim,
And to find *Send in the Clowns*
Appropriately occupies a scale
Even *my* voice can navigate,.

I think I'd love Norwegian summer nights,
just warm enough, yet cool enough
For dreams,
The only season passion is allowed,
The season, even, of intoxication.

I'd love to row a lover in a rowboat
On a windless lake.

I'd settle for
(as Munch had to)
This momentary paradise.

Paul Klee

only Klee could flatten a cathedral
onto a quilted parchment.

only Klee could render
volumetrics musical.

only Klee understood that veiled eyes
are an Arabian song,
a tree is a nose,
and a heart is a spade.

also, her lap is burlap.

he flattened the cobblestone ascent
to the abandoned citadel.

stenographer of structure,
he internalized the shorthand of design.

the father is the mother of the child.
pharaohs, dolls, and deer
(prehistoric, subhistoric)
crowd a picture album
on a single sheet, synchronically,
metaphorically, hieroglyphically:
a collage of our collective imagery.

Klee drew what Yeats imagined.

This Poem Cost Me $1.06

on my way back from paying homage
to Martin Luther King
at his Ebenezer Church,
i do a skillful job of evading and ignoring
panhandlers.
in fact a lot of blacks ask if i need directions
(even though i don't)
and do not even hint at compensation
for their courtesy.

i think it's a southern thing.

but later that day
one slick young guy
does make a hit:

catching me consulting my map
he insists on pointing out
the quickest way back to the Marriott Marquis,
although i'm not really ready to go back yet,
then asks if i can spare
99 cents for a McDonald's burger.

and when i pull a buck from my pocket,
he adds, "and the seven cents for the tax, please."

since he didn't add in a soft drink,
i assume he was going to wash it down
with something that they don't yet purvey
at McDonald's.

ROBERT GRAVES LEFT ENGLAND FOR MALLORCA

I never cared much for the art of Bruce Nauman,
And I am sufficiently Old School to resent
The Cults of Ugliness and Diminishment.

But my opinion was instantaneously altered
Upon reading in The New Yorker
That he and Susan Rothenberg
"go into Santa Fe now and then,
But they steer clear of
The thriving art colony."

Why have we not learned from history
That the individual must shun,
To the extent possible,
Involvement with Collectivists?

What I Learned From Athletic Competition

That you can always do more
Than you (or others) think you can,

And that the human body can produce
Its own chemistry of
Excitement and Tranquility.

And, as a fan, that sports talk can,
Like Literary and Cinematic Criticism,
Philosophy, Theology, or
Sociopolitcal Disputation,

Go beyond Bullshit, Moralizing, and Insult,
To the pleasures of informed, intelligent,
Analytical, creative, experientially grounded, and
Idiomatically diverse yet sophisticated discourse.

In other words: Intellectual Fun.

André Kertész: Circles and Curves

The most obvious of the latter are,
Or course, in his signature photograph of
The *Satiric Dancer*, curled in gleeful
Quasi-bondage on a well-worn sofa in the
Corner of the studio, and flanked,
On trapezoidal walls, by the sculpture of
A twisting male torso - perhaps an ancient
Athlete - and a painting of a bosomy and
Full-hipped naked female. Even the page of
newsprint tacked above her leans with flight
And gravity out of its rectangle.

Sexual attraction is a centripetal force.

You find it also, though, in *Chez Mondrian*,
Where the brimmed hat on the wall,
The vase of yawning flowers, and
The spiral staircase (you are always in a different
Spot yet in a previously traveled longitude)
Controvert the man-made grids for which the resident
Genius grew famous.

Even the cantileverage of the *Eiffel Tower* depends
Upon a Romanesque musculature, whereas the
Rectilinear bridge and building of the *Pont Des Arts*
Is viewed through the transparent circularity of a
Clock whose hour-hand is a gear from which
Extends a star.

The paths of the snowed-in *Washington Square*
Slalom in solitude past the crescent guard-rails.

Every item (every atom) in Kertesz conspires on
Behalf of the organic versus the unyielding:
McDougal Alley disappears beneath the
Tenements: no faces gaze from even the
Best-lit of windows. The snow, now general even

Over Irish-America, will soon be thawed to
Cinders by the 1960s. A fork and its concave shadow
Make praying/preying mantids upon the lip, the lisp,
The shadow of a freshly polished, welcoming,
And pudentatious bowl. The solitary commuters
Between the *Poughkeepsie* tracks have descended
Iron stairs onto a regimented, platformed silence,
Looking past each other towards the insignificance
Of passing, wasted life-time. And on a rainy day in
Tokyo, ties and umbrellas form a snaking queue along
The linearity of Time's relentless, unforgiving arrow.

The *Seine* and *Quais* are parallel commercial
Freeways (bless the resilient Parisians for somehow
Romanticizing the Modern, a feat like rendering
Rotted meat to delicacies, the magic of the
Butcher and the Saucier).

Even the human,
When stretched to sinew
Like the *Underwater Swimmer*,
Has the deathly pallor of the drowned
Upon it.

Only the blown sails of *The Homing Ship*
And the tree which flowers towards infinity of sky
And depths of the reflecting April rainpool
Offer hope of seasonal renewal, that time does
Bend back on itself eternally, as flesh draws
Flesh into its own inexplicable resurrection.

Modest Aspirations

A mistake I've made
At all stages of my life
Is going for the pretty girl
Instead of the Drop-Dead Gorgeous One.

Even when both seem to be
Expressing an interest,
I seem to assume the merely comely one
Will need me more,
Appreciate me more.

Of course this results in the beautiful ones
Being so shocked and downright offended
That they not only write me off forever
But hate my guts eternally as well.

And the merely attractive ones,
Lacking the self-assurance of the beautiful,
Turn out to be insecure, neurotic, jealous,
In need of constant reassurance: what we currently
Refer to as "High Maintenance."

And since, like most writers,
I am, to put it mildly, insecure, neurotic, jealous,
In need of constant reassurance,
And High Maintenance myself,

I either lose these pretty girls
Or end up sorry that
I didn't.

Intro to Biopsychology

I often bring a couple of plays with me
On trips because they're easy to pack
And dialogue can be absorbed
In brief spurts.

This time I bring *Three Tall Women*,
The Play About The Baby,
And *The Coat*.

Edward Albee is such a great playwright,
And there are in any century,
On any continent,
So few plays that endure as literature,
The theatre so often staying at the level
Of entertainment alone.

And Albee, like all great playwrights,
Entertains us by telling us
All the things we do our best
Not to admit to ourselves.

Flying over Upstate

I am not surprised that the worst of the
Turbulence is over my old hometown
Of Rochester, New York. It's known as
The Lake Effect—the result of arctic winds
That are dropped a few additional degrees
Below freezing as they blow over the frozen,
Heavily metallic waters of Lake Ontario.

And passing over Albany,
I can't even re-imagine how cold it felt
Hitchhiking home for Christmas holidays
In 1958 from Worcester, Massachusetts,
Wondering if I and my diminutive classmate
Would ever get a ride or would just turn to ice statues,
Mutt and Jeff (two characters from that era's
Comic pages), extending, Disney-like, our thumbs
At a Thruway on-ramp a little before midnight,
With the mercury holding steady
At 2 degrees below zero, a couple of decades
Before the invention of the Chill Factor.

Somewhere between Syracuse and Rochester,
We trudged to a Howard Johnson's
(or reasonable facsimile)
And emptied our pockets of change
Not for hot coffee, but for a condemned pair's
Last call... to the little guy's parents, who,
When they picked us up two hours later,
Irrationally held me responsible
For having assured their son
That a life without adventure
Was a death-in-life deserving of a
Withering, Heideggerian sneer.

The Versatility of Claude Monet

1.
You think of the Garden of Giverny,
But not of a Poppy Field near it.

You think of "Hollows" as Appalachian.
You think of artists painting peaks and plains
And seas and skies.

But maybe not of gullies we pass by and over.

And yet I've seen,
Through my wife's photographic eye,
The miniature beauties of an Alpine valley,
High in the Rockies or Yosemite,
Inhaling the rarified oxygen
Of Tuolumne or Independence Pass.

2.
The thirty paintings of Rouen Cathedral
At different hours of the light
Remind us why we must yet return
To buildings built as Prayers
Where all that remains of God
Is our nostalgia and His silence.

3.
A tour de force: *La Japonais,* 1876.
They say there is no competition in the arts,
But the Master of Landscapes here tosses off
This random masterpiece
Of textures, folds, and hues,
Coy commentary on itself,
As if to say, "If I so chose,
I could beat every trend at its own game:
In fact, I've just crafted a parody of
An entire cultural obsession
On this single canvas,
And, while I was at it,
Exceeded the skills
Of those that I was poking fun at."

CLAUDE MONET: *THE ARTIST'S GARDEN AT VETHEUIL*, 1881

gardens ordinarily make me uncomfortable:
in nature I prefer *doing* to *looking*,
even if that means looking down at a dusty path
while trudging among magnificent sierra peaks.
i can't picture in memory
most of what I see anyway,
and I don't like squinting at wildflowers
or into the sun,
so I might as well settle for the exercise.
also, french gardens are often so thick
and impenetrable as to leave me on the
outside of the botanical action
looking helplessly in.

but some gardens are better
on the walls of museums and in their
portfolios of color prints,
this one for instance,
the blended, salad splendor of
the greens and sunflowers,
their heliotropic aspirations,
the steep rise of the narrow staircase
towards the domestically triumphant chimney
adding a spume of smoke
to the puffs of cloud
against the azure universe.

strait is the gate,
but infinite the exhalations.

stubby gestural strokes
that anticipate van gogh . . .
and why not . . . vincent's art

was not without its models,
did not spring unfathered
from his mental perturbations.
in the presence of the gardens
haystacks, ponds, and london of
monet, I can simply see,

and I am more alive.

paul klee: *they're biting,* 1920

father and son at the old fishing hole,
which in his case may be the mediterranean.

a cloudless sun is not that bright in klee.
his sun is a lower-wattage bulb.
his sun is a bulb that will soon require replacing.

why shouldn't a fish's fins
point in the wrong direction?
why shouldn't a fish have a face
like milton berle's?
why shouldn't one fish grin
while another merely bears it?

poles and lines will necessarily triangulate,
individually and intersecting.
a family is a triangle
and other shapes that are reducible
to triangles.

boats, bells, and buoys provide a visual distraction
for the fishers, fish, and us.
fishes and fish inhabit radically different worlds,
divided by the base of a right triangle.

klee's fish bite because they
would hate to disappoint.
winslow homer's bite for other reasons.

some fish are smarter than others,
and the less bright claim to be
poor test-takers.

Dalì: *Partial Hallucination, Six Apparitions of Lenin on a Grand Piano*, 1931

Like Anthropomorphic Echo,
It's a great title
(A grand one),

After which I lose interest
And leave it,
And the Andalusian Dog,
And Salvadorable Himself

To the ants.

(Except that I wonder whether he had
As many aunts as I did,

Because punning,
As Freud and Joyce both knew,

Is the key to unlocking
The Unconscious.)

Dalì: *Shirley Temple, the Youngest, Most Sacred Monster On the Cinema in Her Time*, 1939

Her leonine nipples point
In opposite directions.

She has a bat on her head
And a blotchy countenance.

The bones of her victories
Bleach with her upon
The desiccated inland sea.

On the margin,
Garbed in flowing Saharan robes,
She and her shadow skiprope in
Reliquary anonymity.

There is nothing pastoral
About the appearance and disintegration
Of the Earth Mother.

Our impregnation of her will not be
A cleanly, sanitized, cosmetic one.
The soil does not rub off of her.
She swims in black gold.
Her leaking teats show through her halter.
Her belly already bulges a bit.
We must accept her, blood and all.
She is irresistible, like sin itself.

Her nickname is Disorder,
And she ridicules
Our socialistic regimens.

Was Dalì the first to conflate
Hogs and motorcycles,
And perceive in the Mondrianic grids
The triumph of the cybernetic
Over inspiration?

Dalì: *Melancholy, Atomic Uranic Idyll*, 1945

Yes, with or without bombs,
Planes have become depressing again.
Yes, Babe Ruth had twisted them
Out of the ballpark, but it was always
Danny Doppelganger, in his funereal robes,
Whose soft bat whiplashed you
In the bottom of the ninth,
After Mickey Mantle,
On his osteomyelitic pegs,
Had slid into second,
Over the precipice,
Under the volcano,
And into the drink.

Elephants on stilts
Stalk our transitory ecstasies,
And already, within the egg,
The Taj Mahal dwarfs
The Ozymandiacal zygote.

Sonny Rollins at the Cerritos Performing Arts Center

At 76 he makes more changes
In the first thirty-two bars
Than Kenny G will
In his lifetime.

How can a man who can hardly walk
Dance with his sax,
With the complementary trombone,
With drums, percussion, bass guitar?

I don't even like the electric instruments,
But he's arranged his sextet
In and out of generous solos
That allow the guys to show their stuff
But all inside the limits of their talents,
And inside the structure that their leader
Has laid down.

Standards and originals, but nothing oldy-goody,
Nothing too comfortable, nothing too easy
For the audience or himself.

Two hours without an intermission.
A full encore that takes the finale
One flight further.

It's the most intimate though packed performance
I've heard in a concert hall
Since Keith Jarrett at the Royal Festival,
South of Thames,
In spring of 1980.

I haven't heard so many notes
per stitch in time
Since Bird and Diz
Were in their prime.

And what I learn is that I'd better also
Get it back in gear.

A Handy Rejoinder to Have in One's Arsenal

When I mention the collection
Of Edward Field's poems that I have assigned,
I observe a bit of snickering from
A couple of guys in the back row.

And when I say that I consider Field
Our greatest living poet
I observe a glance and smirk
That imply I am probably gay too.

And I have to stop myself from saying to them
What my old pal, Sergeant Roger Hotspur,
An LAPD motorcycle cop,
Used to suggest to anyone who attempted
To impugn *his* sexuality:

"Why don't you send your wife or girlfriend
Up to a cabin at Big Bear with me for the weekend,
And when we get back down
You can ask *her* any questions you may still have
Regarding my sexual orientation."

Hotspur, by the way, loved Field's work too,
Especially Field's characterization of a shark as
"That toothy lurker."

And I have for the two of them
And a few others as well
That stronger-than-sexual affection that
Ironically, has in our age become
The love that dares not speak its name.

The Better Part of Valor

when i was going back to new jersey and
new york for a week to do some
academic moonlighting, I was looking for
the perfect book to savor back in my hotel
room at the end of the work day.

i settled on salman rushdie's *fury*,
because it is set in new york city
and because the author, about my age,
shares many of the concerns – erotic.
familial, international, perennial –
of men of my generation.

although this was only a month after
the tragedy of the world trade center,
i figured i could just pack the controversial
author through in my checked luggage,
so as not to attract the attention of
either terrorists or security personnel.

but the day before leaving,
a horrible thought occurred to me:
what about a hijacking?
after taking us hostages to the middle
of some godforsaken desert,
the hijackers would surely go through our luggage,
which would be tagged with our names.
as if we weren't all in deep doo-doo
to begin with,
my own blasphemous ass would now surely be grass.

beginning to appreciate the neutrality of illiteracy,
i decided to pick up a nice book at the newark airport.

Self-Portrait with a Blue Guitar, 1977

Ever since the romantics
Consecrated the Aeolian Harp as the Consciousness,
Poetry's been music not mimesis.
(Read about it in M. H. Abram's
The Mirror and the Lamp and
Erich Auerbach's *Mimesis.*)

It's a little different for the visual arts,
Which are not linear but spatial
(Read about it in Lessing's *Laocoon.*)

But Wallace Stevens was right:
The blue guitar does subjectively
Order and color
The epiphenomenal reality.

Or did as soon as Whistler started painting London.

Gerald Locklin/New Poems

Stephen Spender, 1969

He seems gracious,
Like a good loser
Of the Super Bowl,

And he seems to have aged
Better than the winner.

And, as with the loser
Of the Super Bowl,

A couple of his best moments
Will always show up

On the highlight reel.

Nicholas Wilder Studying Picasso, Los Angeles, 24ᵗʰ March, 1982

Picasso studied others,
But you can no longer study Picasso:

You can only sell him.

Portraits

At the end of the catalogue
Purchased at the end of the exhibition,

I am as exhilarated
As self-reflexivity,
As intertextuality,
As Indeterminacy,
As the Twentieth Century,

As, I sometimes fear,

The Human Era itself,

Will allow one to be.

Get ready for
The era of
The Oids.

PERSONAL LOANS

Beth Wilson

Personal Loans

PAM'S JUMPING AROUND like she's high on meth, but she doesn't have any scabs on her arms, and her eyes are clear, even though they don't hold still to look at one thing for a second. Maybe she's ADD or something. She looks like a skeleton with skin stretched over it. This isn't the first time she's been in, and Connie saw her coming and disappeared into the back room so I get stuck with her.

"I just need fifty more dollars," she says, swaying from foot to foot. "I can't pay today because I had to help my son pay for his classes. I just need fifty more dollars. Fifty more dollars. Thanks Danielle. You always help me out. You always help me. 'Cause I have to pay for my son's classes. Thanks, Danielle."

I do the paperwork to refinance her loan while she's talking, and give her fifty dollars. After she takes the money, she tells me about helping her son several more times, and finally says she has to catch her bus, and leaves.

"Finally!" Connie says as the door closes behind Pam, and the Christmas sleigh bells we hung on the handle jangle and crash. As if she was the one who Pam was even talking to.

"I know, right?" I stretch. "It makes me tired just watching her."

Sometimes I have to work to keep Connie from getting on my nerves. We're the only two in the office most days, and when you spend that much time with someone, it's important to get along. Even if one person is bitchy and pushy and takes advantage all the time. I do my best to ignore all that, because I need the job.

Since we're together so much, we've had plenty of time to get to know each other. Connie's told me all about her family. She's married to a guy who's five years younger than she is, and she has twin boys who are fourteen. I've told her about my momma's accident with a forklift, and her staying with my baby, Caden, while I work. There's always stories to tell about Caden, because he's two and does the cutest stuff. When Connie talks about her boys, it's always about them getting in trouble or breaking stuff. I hope Caden don't act like that when he's fourteen.

All three of the Personal Loan offices have been busy since the middle of November, so there's not as much time to talk lately. Everybody needs money for the holidays.

Whenever anybody comes in to make a payment, we do our

best to talk them into refinancing, so instead of paying they leave with money in their pockets. Then because of the interest it works out that they owe us a lot more than we gave them.

Connie is in charge, so she's the one who gets to decide when she wants breaks and lunch. I get the leftover times. She wants noon, so I go at eleven. I could go at one, but my favorite soap is on at eleven.

Pretty much the same thing happens every day at lunch. I make sandwiches for me and Momma and Caden, and we eat and watch my soap. Then right before I go back to work, I rock Caden and put him down for his nap.

Caden's a sweet little boy. I didn't have no problems being pregnant with him, which was good since I was finishing high school while I was pregnant. I didn't miss any school for morning sickness, and I got to graduate with the rest of my class. There were at least three of us that were pregnant at graduation, so I didn't stand out that much.

His daddy don't know Caden's his, because we broke up before I found out I was pregnant. Then when he heard, he come and asked if it was his, and I lied and said I'd slept with someone else right after we broke up.

Momma was real mad at me for that because she said we could get child support, but I didn't see how we was going to get child support from a kid right out of high school who lives with his parents. And I didn't want to mess with seeing him anymore, which was why I broke up with him in the first place. That was right before Momma messed up her foot with the forklift at work. If I'd known that was going to happen, I might of tried to get child support.

Anyway, with what I make at Personal Loans, and what Momma brings in from disability, and the bit of help we get from food stamps and WIC, we scrape by.

Momma bitches plenty, though. Especially around this time of year because we don't have much extra for Christmas, and she wants to buy Caden all kinds of presents. Sometimes she acts like she's his momma, and I'm just an aunt or a cousin or something. I gotta say, I'd like to be able to get a couple of presents for Caden. Last year wasn't no big deal because he was just a baby still and didn't know any different. Now he's getting bigger, though, I sure want to be able to buy him some toys and a nice coat. I got him one at one of those clothes give-aways at a church last month, but it isn't very nice. It's all grimy around the sleeves and pockets. I really want to get him a new one.

As soon as I get back in the office from my lunch, Connie grabs her purse and heads out the door.

About one minute after she's gone, Brian's car pulls up. He's the regional manager of all the offices, but he mainly works out of the south office. He visits all the offices every week, though. He comes over pretty much every day now just to see me. He used to do his visits in the afternoon when Connie and me was both here, but one day about a month ago when she was out sick he worked all day with me, and we got pretty tight.

He's married so I don't expect nothing to come of it, but he looks at me like I'm Miss Oklahoma, which makes me feel good.

Brian is old for me, since I'm twenty and he's, like, thirty-five. He's not bad looking, though. He's got straight brown hair that he keeps really short and slicked down. It's getting thin in back, but he doesn't quite have a bald spot yet. He's a little chubby, but he ain't fat. He wears button-down long-sleeve shirts and slacks every day. He says he has to dress up since he's management.

"Hey," I say, smiling at him as he jangles the door open. It isn't one of those smiles I use for customers, but one that shows up on its own just for him. I can't even stop it.

"Hey, yourself," he says back, looking like he just won the lottery or something. He walks over to the counter and leans across it toward me.

I lean forward too, and we have just a little peck of a kiss. He's always trying to get more, but I get too nervous about this stuff at work. I mean, anybody at all could walk in. Or even see us through the glass. He says it don't matter, and he's the one who's married so if he's okay it shouldn't bother me, but I can imagine Connie would be pretty hard to work with if she thought I was having an affair with Brian. She's bitchy enough already.

He's been trying to talk me into going out with him, and I decided last night if he asks me again today I'll say yes. As long as he asks me to do something I want to do. I'm not going to just go hang out with him in a sleazy hotel room.

"How's business?" Brian asks, still on his side of the counter.

"Pretty good," I say, suddenly feeling kind of nervous. I got myself all excited about maybe going out with him, but what if he don't ask this time?

"I'm getting the gifts for the drawing this afternoon," he says. "This year it's going to be giant stockings filled with toys."

I nod. They do the drawing every year. Last year they gave away three whole Christmas dinners, two with giant turkeys and one with a ham. I wonder if he's going to take Connie with him to get the toys. It's the managers that usually go.

He comes around to my side of the counter and pulls me close. "Come in the back with me," he says. "I want to give you something."

"I bet you do," I say, trying to laugh and push him away. I want to go in the back with him, though, so I don't push very hard. It ain't fair that the only guy paying me any attention is one I can't have. If he wasn't married I'd be all over him in one second. But I don't see no point getting involved with someone who isn't going to take care of me.

He pulls Connie's chair over to my desk and gets comfortable, and then he tells me a story about getting into a fight with a customer. I tell him about Pam, but it's hard to focus because he's rubbing on my leg the whole time I'm trying to talk.

"Come in the back with me just for a couple minutes," he says again, when I stop talking.

"This ain't the time or place," I argue.

"Come out with me tonight, then," he says.

It's what I've been hoping he'd say, and now I'm so nervous and excited I feel like jumping up and down and screaming like I might of done in middle school when a boy asked me out. I manage to stay pretty calm on the outside and ask what he has in mind.

"We could get pizza at that place downtown, and then walk around by the river and talk."

I don't know what place he's talking about since I don't ever go downtown, but it sounds pretty romantic, so I tell him okay.

"Really?" He looks shocked for a second, and then he smiles. He leans forward and kisses me on the mouth for a while, until I remember that this isn't a good place to be acting this way. It's hard to pull away from him, though. This is when I start changing my mind about there being no point in messing around with him. The point is because it feels good.

"Connie won't be back for twenty minutes," he says, still just a few inches from my face so that his eyes are all I see. They're bright blue with darker rims, and they look so intense I start thinking maybe he's actually a little bit in love with me. "Come in the back room with me. Please?"

The back room he's talking about is our little breakroom. It has a table and chairs, recliner, refrigerator, sink, and microwave. "Why?" I ask. "I ain't going to have sex with you here."

"I just want to hold you," he says.

I finally give in, and once we get back there we end up having sex after all. I always thought I wouldn't do that, but once I get back there with him kissing my neck and telling me I'm beautiful, I don't want to stop.

By the time Connie gets back, I'm sitting in my chair like I been there the whole time, and Brian is gone off to buy toys for the giant stockings. I'm glad he didn't take her with him.

He shows up later that afternoon as if it's the first time he's been there, and he has a giant stocking for us to hang. It's red with white trim, four feet tall, and big enough around I could put Caden into it. It's all bulgy and out of shape from all the toys. Brian had thought he'd hang it from the wall, but it's so heavy we end up having to prop the foot of it on a little table to support it.

"When are we drawing for it?" Connie asks.

"December twentieth," he says. "We'll have a barrel with all the names in it, and draw for the one at my office first. Then we'll come do yours, and then the north office."

Right before he leaves, when Connie's on a phone call and turned the other way, he gives me a little hug and a kiss on top of the head.

There's only an hour left before I go home, but it drags, and I feel about as jumpy as Pam. I start wishing I hadn't told Brian he could pick me up. My momma won't like it that he's married. Or if I don't tell her she'll start expecting him to marry me. And if that isn't a problem, she won't like it that he's closer to her age than mine. She's only three years older than he is.

As soon as I get home I tell her about the whole thing, and she gets a little huffy, but she actually seems kind of pleased that I got a date, even if it's with an old married guy.

"Just don't get too attached to him," she warns. "If he'll cheat on his wife, he'll cheat on you."

I think this is probably good advice, but the truth is I been getting more attached every day, and it's real hard to get less attached once you're already more attached.

When he comes to the door, Momma answers it because I'm in the bathroom finishing up my makeup. I can hear them talking, so I hurry. Even if she's acting nice about me dating him, who knows what awful thing she might say by accident.

I come out of the bathroom and his face lights up at seeing me, and mine feels like it might be glowing from seeing him, too, and he gives me a little hug and kiss like he can't even help himself. Then I get my coat and give Caden a kiss and we leave.

Downtown turns out to be fun, with lots of restaurants and tall buildings lit up with Christmas lights, and the riverwalk decorated pretty and the river flowing black with the lights all reflected in it. The weather isn't exactly cold yet, and the buildings block the worst of the wind.

After we eat, when we're walking around looking at the lights and the buildings and the people, he takes my hand, and I notice he's not wearing his wedding ring. For some reason that makes me feel special.

"So what did you tell your wife?" I ask. I had meant to keep my mouth shut on it and not bring her up, but the truth is I'm dying to know. I don't really know much about her. Even though he's talked about leaving her, he hasn't actually said anything bad she's done, or what she's like.

"She was going over to her sister's to do some craft shit, so I said I'd find something to do."

"Oh." That doesn't really give me any clues, and I start to feel sad that I'm liking him so much but it's probably not going to go anywhere.

"Hey," he says, stopping and pulling me up against him.

"What?" I lean my head against his chest and don't look up at him because I'm still feeling sad.

"Hey," he repeats, putting his finger under my chin and gently tilting my head up so we're facing each other. He kisses me for a bit, and then smiles. "It'll be okay," he says.

The kissing makes me feel all warm and fuzzy inside, but I know deep down it won't be okay. Still, I don't want to mess up what I have by thinking about something that hasn't happened yet. I smile at him like I believe him and we walk some more.

He doesn't try to get me to have sex with him. When he takes me home he gives me a hug and a sweet kiss that doesn't seem like it's asking for anything.

"Thanks for dinner," I say.

"Thanks for going out with me."

After I go inside I wonder if this is a beginning or if it's an ending. Either way, at least I had a good evening.

I don't see him again until Monday, but he don't come in until afternoon when Connie's there, like he did before we started messing around. I'd sat there all through the noon hour wondering if he was going to come in, and then getting used to the idea that he wouldn't. It's not easy, and I feel like crying.

When he does finally come in, he acts like nothing ever happened at first. Then the phone rings and Connie answers it, and he leans over and says he'd like to see me again.

After spending the last couple of hours feeling heartbroke, I have to hesitate and think about it. I mean, it'll just get worse, and having a little taste of it makes me think it might not be worth it. I look up into his eyes, and they change from being flirty to being thoughtful and, maybe, understanding.

"We'll talk about it later," he whispers.

Then he stands up straighter and more business-like, and starts asking me about accounts and such in a normal voice.

I don't know what I figured he meant when he said later, but apparently he means right after work. When I get home he's parked in front of my apartment, and he gets out of his car as soon as he sees me.

"I'm sorry," he says right away.

"What for?" I don't say this coldly or to make him feel bad, but I really don't know why he's apologizing. He never promised he'd come by at lunch, so he wasn't standing me up. It was my own stupid fault for expecting too much.

"This whole thing," he said. "I shouldn't be asking you out and getting you to sleep with me when I can't give you anything."

"You mean 'cause you're married."

He nods and looks sad.

It's the sad look that messes me up. I thought I would just tell him it's better for us to be friends and go our separate ways, but he looks so miserable that instead I tell him that I don't want him to give me anything, and just getting to spend time with him is enough for me.

He keeps looking at me for a few more seconds before he smiles and gives me a hug. "You're amazing," he says.

I don't feel like I'm amazing, but I'm not sorry he thinks so. And it feels real good to be in his arms again, when I was thinking a few hours ago that I wouldn't get to be anymore. When I go inside, it don't even bother me that my momma is bitching again about how we don't have enough money. I don't know what she expects me to do about it. I can't hardly get another job, and I already work overtime on Saturdays.

Next day at lunch after a visit to the back room, Brian pulls Connie's chair over next to mine and we sit and talk. He tells me he can't leave his wife right now because it would ruin him financially.

I tell him I understand, even though I don't. It makes me feel bad that he keeps trying to explain why he can't be with me. I'd lots rather have him talk about what we can have, even if that's only lunchtimes and sometimes a date on a weekend.

"What do you want for Christmas?" he asks.

I shake my head. I don't want him getting me anything when I can't give him anything, and I tell him so.

He presses his lips together in a line like he's thinking about it, but he doesn't argue, and he doesn't bring it up again.

The closer Christmas gets the more it bothers me that I can't get much for Caden. Since Momma's been bitchin' about it for weeks, I hate to bring it up to her, but I do, and we sit down and try to figure out a way to buy him something.

"Why don't you just take a little bit from a couple of customers?" Momma says. "Say someone brings in a payment of fifty dollars, and you just put in that they paid forty-five, and keep that five. They won't miss that five dollars. I bet most people don't keep track, anyhow."

"If I get caught I'd get fired, though," I argue. "Then I wouldn't have any money. That ain't worth the risk."

She sighs. "Well, I saved back ten dollars from the last two checks, and that's the best I could do."

"I saved back ten, too," I tell her, feeling pleased that I saved as much as she did. It wasn't easy. "What do you figure we can get him for twenty dollars? Should we get him a toy? Or a decent coat?"

She shakes her head. "That coat you got him at that church is practically rags. I wish people wouldn't give shit away that should go in a trash can. I say we get him a coat."

"What are we going to do when he gets bigger, Momma?" I ask, feeling like I might cry, all of a sudden.

"We just do the best we can."

"How did you take care of me when I was little and you didn't have no help?"

She shrugs. "Your daddy didn't leave until you were seven. By that time you were in school all day, so I didn't have to pay for daycare. Once Caden starts school, I'll find a part time job that don't require me standing a lot, and it'll be easier. I can still get my disability as long as I don't work more than twenty hours a week."

I nod. We'll do better once both of us are working. It's still three years away, but it's something.

We go out and find a good coat at Wal-Mart that's just fifteen dollars. We get it a couple of sizes too big so he can wear it next year, too. Then we find a little car that's just a dollar, and a tube of red and green holiday M & Ms. It ain't much, but I feel a lot better having something to give him.

Brian comes over on Friday to take me to a movie. It's been a long time since I been to a movie, and I'm almost as excited about that as I am to go on a date with Brian. He's in jeans and a t-shirt this time, but he looks almost as dressed up as when he's wearing slacks and a button-down.

This time when he gets here I'm ready, but when I open the door he comes on in anyway, and sits down on the couch and makes himself at home. It's a little weird, but maybe he thinks he needs to impress my momma or something. I sit down next to him, almost but not quite touching his leg.

He asks Momma how she's doing, and she says she's okay. I'm glad she doesn't start telling him all about her foot. I've told him basically what happened, but when she starts talking about the way the forklift separated her heel right off, it's enough to make a body sick. Even after all the physical therapy, she still limps a lot, and she uses a cane or a motorized cart whenever we go to the store. It's because of that she's put on so much weight. She used to be skinnier even than me.

Caden comes over and climbs into Brian's lap and tells him about Barney, which is cute as anything but I worry a little bit that he might be getting bored. I wonder if he really doesn't mind having my kid crawling all over him, or if he's just being polite.

As soon as Caden pauses, I ask Brian if he's ready to go.

"Sure," he says, standing up and setting Caden carefully on the floor. If I didn't already know he isn't around kids much, I'd know by the way he holds Caden like he thinks he'll break him.

On the way to the movie he asks me how come we don't have a tree up, and I tell him Caden would just tear it down again so we're waiting 'til next year.

"Are you the kind that puts up lights and stuff in the yard?" I ask.

"My wife doesn't let me," he says. "She has a certain way she does all the inside, and then we hire someone to come hang the lights on the outside."

I wonder how she keeps him from doing anything he wants to do. Does she scream at him? Threaten to leave? Throw things? Or maybe she's just super-bitchy like Connie, and she wears him down with it until he don't even want to do things anymore. If I ever find a guy I love enough to marry and live with, I swear I'm not going to do that to him.

He takes me to the big theater downtown, and we sit in the back and make out for most of the movie. I don't even know what the movie was about when we leave.

"Wanna walk around for a while?" he asks, taking my hand and pulling me close to him. "It's not too cold."

The weather is pretty nice, cool and dry, so I nod and lean into him and we walk around.

"I need to ask you something," he says, after a few minutes of just walking.

I'm feeling all warm and secure and totally in the moment until he says that, but the words start a little chill going down my spine.

"Okay," I say, hoping it's something I don't mind answering.

"How are you fixed for Christmas?" he asks.

He knows from talking to me the last few weeks that I don't have much money right now, but even so I don't want to tell him how bad things are.

I shrug. "We're pretty much done with our shopping," I say, feeling proud of the way I didn't say what he wants to hear.

He doesn't say anything for a while, and I'm just starting to think we're done with it when he pulls me off the path and leads me over to a bench to sit down. The metal is cold through my jeans.

"Do you trust me?" he asks.

This is totally out of the blue, and I don't know what to say.

Of course I don't trust him. He's the kind of guy who cheats on his wife.

But I like him. I want him. I want him to want me.

But I can't say any of that.

It's all very confusing, and I can't think of anything I can say.

He sighs. "That's fair. I guess what I really wanted to say is that you can tell me stuff. I won't judge you or talk about anything you say with anybody else."

In my experience, someone only says they won't judge you when they think there's something about you to judge. Which means they already judged you.

"What are you talking about?" I say, starting to feel defensive.

His eyes get big, almost like he's afraid. "No, don't take it that way," he says. "All I'm trying to say is, I know you don't make a lot of money, and I'd like to do something to help you for Christmas."

I relax a little. Just a little. "I don't need no help," I insist.

"I know you don't want me to give you something," he says. "But what if you could win that stocking of toys for Caden?"

Now he has my attention. "Don't the winners' names get posted up at the office where they win?" I ask.

He nods. "We'd have to fix it. But it wouldn't be too hard."

It's a little bit like my momma's idea, except with this idea I wouldn't get fired. Especially not with the regional manager hooking me up. I smile at him. "That would be pretty cool, then."

The next week, a couple of days before the drawing, Brian tells me to pick out a customer from my office who I think would definitely not be able to visit his office in the next two or three weeks while the name is posted.

I immediately think of Pam, with her nervous jumping and her eyes that never stop moving. She walks or takes the bus, so there's no way she's traveling all over town.

On the twentieth, he doesn't come in until afternoon when it's time for the drawing. It turns out to be a lot less of a deal than I had imagined. Brian has a box with a bunch of folded up pieces of paper in it. He shakes it around and holds it out to Connie; she pulls a piece of paper out and reads it out loud. The name don't sound familiar to me. She types it into the database of customers and gets the phone number and calls.

"Well, that was kind of dumb," she says after she hangs up the phone.

"What?" Brian asks.

"It was an old lady and she said she doesn't need any toys. She'd rather just have her fuckin' loan paid off."

Brian's eyes widen slightly in surprise, and then he shrugs. "You can't please some people," he says.

"Yeah. No kidding."

That evening when I get home Brian's car is in front of my apartment. He gets out when he sees me and pops open his trunk.

"How do you want to do this?" he asks. "You want to sneak it in so Caden won't know about it 'til Christmas Day?"

I agree and go in ahead of him so I can have Momma take Caden in the kitchen until we get the stocking into my room. Brian only sticks around for a couple of minutes after that, and then he says he's got a party his wife's making him go to, so he better go home and get ready.

Momma shakes her head once the door's closed behind him. "That ain't gonna last," she says.

"His marriage?" I say hopefully. But I know better.

She keeps shaking her head. "His affair with you, Hon. It ain't gonna last."

I scowl at her, wishing I could slap her for bringing it up now, when I was feeling so good. "Why do you say that?"

"I've known a lot of cheating men in my day," she says. "I can just tell."

We both know she's right, and my chest starts aching with keeping it inside.

"I gotta see what's in that stocking," I say, heading to my room so she don't see me trying not to cry.

The second I'm by myself the tears bust out of me, and I have to hold a pillow over my face to keep it quiet. It ain't just the idea of giving up Brian I'm crying for. It's the why of it. It's because I know the reason he won't leave his wife. She might be bitchy, but she takes care of stuff for him, and she makes lots of money, and she knows people who throw fancy parties.

The truth is, I'm not good enough for him.

It don't stop hurting, but after a while I can't cry anymore. I sit up and blow my nose and wait for my breathing to get back to normal. I don't mean to keep thinking about him, but I can't help remembering the way his face lights up when he sees me, or how his eyes seem like they get darker when he's looking right into mine. He does love me, I think. It ain't enough, but it's something.

When I'm all calm again, I grab the foot of the stocking and hold it up so the toys fall out on the bed. Right away I get a sinking feeling in my middle 'cause I see it's mostly big kid toys. I can't give that shit to Caden 'cause he might choke on the pieces. It even says so on the boxes. I should of guessed Brian wouldn't know how to pick out kids' toys.

I dig through the pile and decide Caden probably can't do much damage with the Nerf football and the robot dinosaur, so I can at least give him those. There's an electronic solitaire game that I figure Momma will enjoy. She'll be surprised to get something. I put those in my underwear drawer to wrap up later, and then start cramming the rest back into the stocking. Maybe I'll just save it all for when Caden's older.

There's a little box of Legos with a racecar on it that I keep out for me. After I chuck the stocking into the back corner of my closet, I open the box and pull out the bag of tiny pieces.

It don't look exactly like the picture when I finish, and there's a couple of leftover pieces. I don't see where I went wrong, though. I set it up on my dresser and throw away the box and the extra pieces. It still looks like a car, anyways.

How to Move On

Beth Wilson/Personal Loans

AS JASON TURNED LEFT onto Ballerina Drive, the late afternoon sun hit the windshield straight on so that, with all the dirt on the glass, it was almost impossible to see. The hottest part of the day was over, and the main street of the trailer park was full of half naked children riding bikes and scooters and rollerblades.

Most Fridays, we'd be home from cleaning houses before four, but that day the second house took longer than normal because we'd had a fight. I kept my head turned toward the window, still feeling angry, but for the first time in a while, feeling hopeful, too.

When we'd gone to the Smiths' house after lunch, it was just as nasty as it always was. The kitchen counter was covered with dried food, and the floor crunched under our shoes. In the living room, newspapers and paper plates caked with moldy food blanketed the couches and the coffee table. Dirty socks and knee high pantyhose were scattered across the floor. Nobody looking at that mess would guess these people were brilliant.

Jason grabbed a 30 gallon lawn bag from under the sink and began throwing away the trash in the living room. I piled dishes in the sink and sprayed the countertops down with disinfectant to loosen up the petrified food so I could scrape it up. The Smiths' house was pretty gross, but we were used to it, and we had a system. We'd been cleaning houses together for over a year, and I'd done it by myself for several years before that. We usually finished in about two hours.

After the kitchen, I headed into the master bedroom to clean the little bathroom in there. I expected it to be gross, too, but this time the mess surprised me.

There was shit everywhere. Literally. It didn't look fresh, either. I stared for a few seconds, wondering how they managed to get it up on the walls so high. Did the toilet explode? Was it some kind of plunging incident? And how long had it been there? Did they keep using it after they made the mess?

One thing I knew. There was no way I was going to clean that. The money wasn't worth it.

I closed the bathroom door, sat down on the bed, and folded my arms across my chest, furious. How could anyone leave something like that and not be embarrassed to have someone see it, even the housekeepers? Didn't we count as people? The answer to that was obviously "no," and that made me even more furious.

Jason walked into the bedroom spraying furniture polish on a rag, the feather duster sticking out of his back shorts pocket like a perky bird tail. "What's wrong?"

"You won't believe the bathroom."

"Worse than normal?"

"Take a look." I waved at the bathroom door.

He put down the polish and rag and opened the bathroom door, and then looked back at me, half wincing, half grinning. "Sucks to be you."

I would've felt the same way if he'd had the bathrooms, so I didn't take it wrong. Anyway, he was just trying to lighten me up a little. After a minute of pouting, I got up and sprayed it all down with disinfectant, turned on the fan and shut the door on the mess again. This house was worth two hundred dollars a month. We couldn't afford to lose that much money.

"It isn't fair."

He shrugged. "People are pigs."

As if that made it okay. As if he had a right to expect me to spend my whole life cleaning up after pigs so that we could afford to live in a trailer park.

When I'd started, it hadn't seemed so bad. In fact, at first I'd been so excited about how much money I could make, I'd bragged about my "career." That was when I was nineteen, right after we got married. I'd had two semesters of junior college by that time, and had been bored with it. I was ready for "real life." That was before I learned that real life involved so much shit.

"I can't do this forever," I said. "I can't! I'm tired of getting treated like dirt. I'm tired of wiping up people's shit. This isn't me!"

"Who are you, then?" Jason asked. "The fucking Queen of England?"

"I don't know who I am," I said. "But I'm not a fucking maid!"

"You shouldn't let your job define you," he said. "It's a job. We do it and go home."

"It's not just a job! It's boring, and gross, and it's sucking the life out of me to spend my days this way!"

"Quit, then," Jason said. His voice was getting sharper now; I was pulling him into the fight. "Go find a job running a cash register. And enjoy working evenings and weekends for minimum wage. I'm not working at a grocery store again!"

Jason worked at a grocery store when we met, and had

until last year when they fired him, after his foot surgery made it impossible to stand in one place for several hours. It was true they'd done him wrong, and I didn't want him to have to go back to it. But what I hated was how he always assumed there were only two options: clean houses or work at a grocery store. That wasn't going to work for me.

"Or we could go to college and learn how to do something. We could get real jobs making real money." I stood up and threw my arms wide. "Money like these people have."

"Money isn't everything," he said, turning his back to me.

"It is if you don't have it," I said bitterly.

Money was big houses, and nice cars, and health insurance, and vacations, and dinners at restaurants, and movies, and all the stuff we didn't have. Money was freedom from the trap where we had to clean up messes like this so we could live in our stupid little trailer park on the wrong edge of town.

"I'm not a college type," he said evenly, keeping his back to me. "I tried it once already, remember?"

"You were working sixty hours a week last time you tried to go to school. That doesn't really count." I was so sick of this argument. He said his lines, I said mine. It was boring, but I was so angry with him I couldn't stop myself. If I could just make him see I was right, everything would be okay. If I couldn't, I didn't know what I was going to do. Explode, maybe.

He was tired of the argument, too. He gave me a dirty look, shook his head and started feather dusting the edges of the overflowing bookshelves.

"How am I supposed to keep believing in you when you don't even believe in yourself?" I shouted.

He kept his back to me and didn't answer.

My whole life seemed like a waste of time. There was nothing important in it at all.

After that, we didn't talk while we cleaned. It was pointless to try to talk to him, anyway. He didn't think he deserved better, but I knew I did. Maybe I wasn't the fucking queen of anything, maybe I wasn't any kind of genius, but maybe I was something. If he wouldn't go to school, maybe I would. Maybe get a Political Science degree. Or History. I'd liked those classes when I went to school before.

I didn't know what I would do, exactly, or where I would end up. But I would find myself. With or without Jason.

He turned off the radio when we got in the car, which was a sure sign he wanted to talk, but I turned to the window and refused to even look at him.

Maybe hopeful was too strong of a word for how I felt at that moment, as we pulled into the trailer park. Maybe it was more of a grim satisfaction. I had a plan, of sorts. Or at least, a resolution.

"Police car," Jason said as he got close to our driveway.

I looked up, interested in spite of myself. I didn't want to care who called the police on who this time, but the little dramas of our neighborhood were the only entertainment I had. It was in front of Steve and Tammy's doublewide this time, almost directly across the street from ours.

As Jason pulled the car into our driveway, I turned around in my seat so I could watch the cop helping Steve into the backseat of the police car.

Steve was only, like, twenty. He had a schizo issue he was supposed to take pills for, but he usually smoked pot instead. Most of our neighbors smoked pot, at least a little, but Steve and Tammy smoked a lot. I wondered how the cop didn't notice the smell. I could smell their house from the middle of the street.

I took my bucket of cleaners and dirty rags into the laundry room as soon as I got in the house so they wouldn't stink. I'd started out my cleaning "career" thinking people would have their own supplies, but then I found out they expected me to dust with their old underwear – complete with skidmarks – or clean the entire house with nothing but a bottle of Windex, so I started bringing my own bucket of basic supplies.

Before I had the washing machine going, I heard the front door open. When I went into the living room, Tammy was perched on the edge of the futon talking to Jason. She was cute and thin, with big boobs barely contained by a wifebeater, and gossip was that she never wore panties under her stretched out boxers.

I thought about saying hi and going on through the living room to the bedroom, where I'd left the book I was reading. Jason could always catch me up on the drama after Tammy left. But I did wonder, a little, what had happened. I sat down in the recliner across from her and put on what I hoped was a politely interested and caring face.

"I didn't want to call the cops," Tammy said, her hand fluttering nervously around her mouth like she had a phantom cigarette, or maybe a roach. She didn't ask if she could smoke, though. Everybody knew they couldn't smoke in our house because of my allergies.

"What happened?" Jason said sympathetically. He was practically the neighborhood therapist.

"He got out of control. He hasn't taken his pills in two weeks. Then he quit going to work three days ago."

"Probably because of all the pot." I sounded a little harsh, even to myself. Jason and Tammy both scowled at me, in case there was any doubt I'd misspoken.

"Then what happened?" Jason prompted. He might as well have said, "Please ignore my wife." Ugh.

"Yesterday he started yelling and throwing stuff, and I was afraid he would hurt Dalton, so I went ahead and called the police."

"Where's Dalton now?" I shouldn't have said anything, again, but I couldn't help worrying about him, even though I wasn't the maternal type. He was only two, and he spent about half his time at Tammy's mom's, and the other half shut up in his bedroom.

"He's taking his nap," Tammy said, shooting me another dirty look.

"By himself?"

"He's okay in his crib." She was obviously pissed, now. "He'll sleep until five." She started twisting her hair and tried to look sad instead of angry. "I hate when Steve's gone."

"They'll get him straightened out and home in no time," Jason said kindly. It made me want to hit him over the head, the way he was pandering to her stupid story.

I wished I'd gone on to the bedroom after all. Now Jason was going to yell at me for being rude to her, and her story was so dumb she didn't even care about it. What a waste of time.

I tuned out and started daydreaming about school. Maybe after I got my degree, I could teach high school. Would I like teaching? I tried to imagine myself standing in front of a roomful of teenagers. Hmm. Maybe. I fingered the frayed edge of one of the holes in my jeans. If I had a job like that, I could wear nice clothes, instead of holey jeans and stained t-shirts.

"Do you guys have any Lortabs?" Tammy asked, breaking up my daydream. "My back is really giving me fits, and I can't go back to the doctor until after payday. I can give you three dollars a pill, if you have a couple."

"All I have is regular strength ibuprofen," Jason told her.

"I'll sell those to you for three dollars a pill if you want, though."

She didn't look amused. When it came to pills, she didn't joke around. "I guess I'll run up the street and ask Melody or somebody." She frowned and stood up.

Jason stood up, too. "Good luck," he said. "Sorry about Steve."

She shrugged. "His dad'll probably bail him out."

So much for the drama. As soon as Tammy was out the door, I went into the bedroom to find my book. With any luck, Jason wouldn't yell at me for being rude, and I wouldn't yell at him for settling.

Jason followed me into the bedroom and stood in the doorway staring at me, apparently not aware that it was a bad choice. We were together 24/7. Why couldn't he give me any space?

I flopped down on my side of the bed and picked up my book, hoping he'd take the hint.

"You didn't have to be rude to Tammy because you're mad at me," he said, putting his hands on his hips.

"I'm not mad at you. But it seems like it should bother you that our pothead neighbor locks her baby up and leaves the house."

"It does, but he's probably better off with her than at some foster family where he'll get abused. At least she loves him."

He had a point. It was probably why the cops left him there. I held the book up higher so I couldn't see him, even though I was too disgusted to focus on reading.

"If you're not mad, then why are you hiding behind that book?"

Because I can't stand the sight of you anymore. But I didn't want to go there. I mean, I didn't want to leave him. I just didn't want to be with him every single minute. "I'd really like a little time by myself," I said.

"I think we need to talk about it," he said. "I don't like when you're mad at me."

"I think we're all talked out," I said, lowering the book. "Unless you want to change your position."

He sighed. "I can compromise, I guess. I mean, maybe something else will come along. I'll get a paper on Sunday and look for a different job."

"You'd have to work twice as much for half the money, remember?" I set my book down, sat up, and sighed. "It doesn't matter. If you can't pull yourself together and do something with your life, then I'll do something else with mine."

"Is that a threat?" His lips tightened, and his eyes narrowed.

It was his mad face, but it occurred to me that he looked more scared than mad. He was a big coward. I was letting a coward tell me how to live my life. But maybe I had been a coward for allowing it.

"You don't have to go to school. But I do. I'm going to school. I'm going to make something of my life." I really could do this. I didn't have to wait for my husband to make my life better; I'd do it on my own.

He stood there with his arms crossed and his face all scowled up for so long I wondered if he was going to cry or something. Finally, though, he uncrossed his arms and came over and sat down next to me.

"If I try again, and I don't make it, are you going to think I'm stupid and look for somebody better?"

I studied him. Did that mean he was giving in? Did I win?

"I won't look for somebody better," I said cautiously, "but I still want to go to school, whether you do or not."

"Okay," he said, uncrossing his arms and sitting down on the bed. "If it means that much to you, then I'll give it one more try. On Monday as soon as we're done cleaning, let's go to the junior college and get the information we need to get started."

"Really?" I couldn't believe he'd agreed, just like that. After all the fights and screaming, I finally won?

"Just promise me a couple of things," he said.

Of course there was a catch. Of course there was. "What?"

"I can't go to school and work. If you want me to go to school, you're going to have to help me. Let me go and get my degree, and then when I'm done, I'll support you while you get yours."

Four more years of being a fucking maid while he got to go to school? No way was I going to do that.

But this was a big step for him, so I'd give him a little time to get used to it before we went on to the next step. Maybe give him a semester to realize that it wasn't as hard as he was making it out to be. I could wait one more semester.

"Okay," I said.

"Okay."

"Was there another thing?" I asked, when he didn't say anything else. "You said a couple of things."

"Just don't leave me," he said. "I couldn't stand it if you left me."

"Okay," I said. That one was easy enough. "I won't leave you."

"Okay," he said again.

"Are we done, then? Is it all right if I read my book?" What I really meant was, "Would you please leave me alone, now?"

He got the hint, sighed and nodded, and went into the kitchen to start supper.

Since it was Friday night, it wasn't long after supper that someone knocked on the door. Everybody in the park got together on Friday nights. It was just a matter of who and where. Which depended on who was fighting and who were BFFs. It changed every day. Jason peeked out the window.

"It's Bobby. What do you want to do?"

"Well, I don't want to go to his house. It stinks." Bobby and Shelly had three cats.

"So it's okay if everybody ends up here?" His hand was on the doorknob.

The bad thing about that was that I couldn't leave if it got boring. Some weekends, there wasn't enough beer in the world to make our friends interesting. But sometimes we had fun. I sighed. "Whatever. Ask Bobby to buy some of the beer, though. We don't have the money to buy for everyone."

Jason opened the door and Bobby sauntered in. "'sup?" he asked, nodding at me.

I liked Bobby, in spite of his faux ghetto outfit and attitude. He was our age—twenty-six—but he seemed younger.

"You guys doing anything?" I asked him.

"Can't do much. Shelly lost her job again, so money's tight." Bobby flopped onto the futon, slouching down low.

"When did she lose this one?" Jason asked, pulling beer out of the fridge for the three of us. "I thought she just started it."

"She had this one all of two weeks." Bobby shook his head. "She's going through 'em faster and faster."

"She needs to stop looking for jobs in daycare," I said. Shelly cussed more than a fifteen-year-old boy.

"I know. I try to tell her, but she gets so upset." He shook his head again and took a long drink.

I knew why. She wanted kids more than anything, but she'd had parts of her ovaries removed. So far that year she'd had three miscarriages. I wasn't sure if I wanted kids or not yet, but I couldn't imagine trying over and over like that and losing them.

"Where is she?" Jason asked. "Coming over?"

"She went with Tammy to get some munchies. They'll be back pretty soon."

"Did Tammy get some pills?" I asked.

"Prob'ly." Bobby shrugged. "She's out of it."

"What about Dalton?" I asked, feeling anxious.

"Her mom came and got him," he said.

I nodded, relieved. Bobby and Shelly's trailer was beside Tammy and Steve's, the front and back doors only a few feet apart, so they always knew what was going on, even when Tammy and Shelly were enemies, which was about half the time.

We sat around and watched TV for a while until Jason got up and went to the refrigerator for another beer. "Last one. Time for a beer run," he announced.

We piled into our car and headed to the gas station on the corner. Jason started to grab the biggest case of bottled beer out of the cooler, but I nudged him and scowled, and he picked up the twelve-pack of cans instead, sticking his tongue out at me so I would know he was annoyed, but not mad.

Bobby had been standing back like he was just along for the ride until he saw the twelve-pack. He frowned, and then reached into the cooler and got another one. I waited until he was in front of us and gave Jason an "I-told-you-so" look. I didn't usually get to be right twice in one day. It was a good feeling.

When we got back, Tammy and Shelly were sitting on Tammy's front steps eating tacos. Before we were out of the car, they were headed across the street.

"What'd you bring us?" Shelly asked.

"Nothing for you," Jason joked.

"I guess I'll take yours then, dick." She punched him on the arm.

"Hey." Jason grabbed her wrist and twisted her arm. Even as patient as he was, he didn't like her talking to him that way. "Be nice, or you get nothing."

"Fine, fine. I'm sorry," she said. But she laughed.

"Heard anything from Steve?" I asked Tammy. Her eyes were flat. She'd definitely found some pills somewhere. I wondered if she got them around here, or if her mom brought them. Her mom worked for a doctor.

"Yeah. His dad called. They took him to the hospital instead of jail. He'll probably have to stay in psych for a while 'til they get his meds fixed." She looked at the two cases of beer. "So, we gonna party or what?"

We went inside, and Bobby turned on the radio. It was on a country station, since that's what we listened to, mostly. Jason grabbed my hand and started swinging me around the living room. He was a good dancer and I was terrible, but he didn't let that slow him down. Before we got halfway through the song, though, Bobby flipped the station to rock. He didn't like country music so much. It didn't work with his ghetto image.

Jason switched gears in mid-step to match the song, and I did my best to follow him.

"You need more to drink, Kim," Bobby said, laughing.

"People always say that when I dance," I complained. But at least I was having fun.

Shelly grabbed Bobby's hand and they started dancing, too, and we danced until a commercial came on the radio.

"Beer break!" Bobby yelled, and grabbed cans from the fridge and passed them out to everybody. We all sat down, and then Jason started telling them about the Smiths' bathroom.

"That's sick, man," Bobby said. "Rich people are gross."

"There are gross poor people, too," I said. "It doesn't have anything to do with how much money they have."

Jason shook his head. "They're gross, and they're snobs. They think they're better than everybody else."

That was the ultimate sin in Jason's book. Nobody had the right to think they were better than anybody, and especially him. "Whatever," I said. I'd already won, and I didn't need to defend the Smiths, anyway. They were rich geniuses. "To be fair, though, some of our clients are really nice."

"Some of them," Jason agreed. "But what about the clients who forget to pay us but make us come get the check? Or the clients who won't let us park our car in their driveway? Where's the respect?"

"All right! Fine! Rich people are assholes," I said. But I still wanted to be one. I wanted a nice house, and a nice car, and a nice job. Why was that wrong?

"I need some fresh air," I said, standing up.

What I meant was that I wanted to be by myself for a few minutes, but they didn't take hints very well. Everybody else stood up when I did and followed me outside.

The tip of the sun was still visible on the other side of the manager's office up the street; the sky to the east was dark, though. I had intended to sit down on the porch swing, but I heard people playing guitars and singing and headed that direction instead.

On an empty lot a ways down the block, there were about twenty people sitting around on blankets, plastic lawn chairs, and folding camp chairs. Most of them I recognized, but the two guys playing guitars and the girls sitting next to them must've been somebody's friends from somewhere else. A bug light hung from a low branch of a tree, and a cooler sat at the base of its trunk. I found a spot on a blanket spread across the prickly yellow grass, and someone handed me a beer.

Jason sat down next to me and put his arm across my shoulders and joined in the singing. He had a good voice. I leaned into him and put my ear against his chest, feeling the vibrations of the song as he sang.

It was still warm out, but there was a little bit of a breeze every once in a while, so it wasn't too bad. I looked up at the sky through branches and the dark outlines of the surrounding trailers. Ballerina Drive was far enough from the city lights that you could see the stars. The moon was a thin sliver, resting on its back, but it was bright enough you could see the rest of it in shadow.

I could tell this would be one of those Friday nights that everybody talked about for weeks afterward and tried desperately to re-create. It never worked to remake old ones, though. That's what the people around here didn't get. They didn't know how to move on.

The One Who's Moving

T HE WHOLE TRAILER PARK has been pretty quiet the last few months. It seems like everybody's moving away. There are twenty-four lots on Ballerina Drive, the main street of the park. They all used to be full, but now there are only seven trailers left. In a trailer park when people leave, they take their houses with them. So the quiet feeling has an emptiness that's different than a regular block of empty houses.

People and their houses have been moving in and out ever since Kim and I moved in, going on five years ago, but I notice the emptiness a lot more this summer. Probably because Kim moved out in March, so my house is empty, too. Plus, I'm home a lot more this summer than I ever have been. Since she left, I haven't been able to find a job.

We cleaned houses together for two years, and then Kim insisted that I should go to school, so I just helped her out a couple of days a week and went to school the other three. I never thought I could do it, but I guess it wasn't as bad as I thought. She was supposed to wait to start school until I finished, but that didn't happen either. She started school in January, and took off with some guy in March. Even though I was still helping her out with the cleaning, she took all the clients. She offered to let me keep some, but they wanted her.

I've been doing odd jobs since school let out, while I'm waiting for one of those hundreds of applications I've put in all over town to pay off, but even those have trickled down to nothing. I haven't had any kind of work at all in nearly two weeks.

Normally on a day like today, when there's nothing to get out of bed for, I wouldn't bother getting out of bed until at least noon, but for some reason I wake up at eight-thirty, and after about an hour I get tired of trying to go back to sleep.

It's a Wednesday in July. On Monday I applied for every job I could pretend I qualified for in the Sunday paper, and yesterday I drove around to a bunch of the places I applied to in the last three weeks, just to remind them I exist. But nobody's calling.

All I have left in my pantry is tuna and canned spaghetti. Maybe today the Morenos will get home from the lake, and I can go over there for supper. They didn't say how long they would be gone when they left.

It might be kind of crazy over there, with all their kids—seven-year-old Emily, five-year-old Landon, and twin boys still in diapers—but it's peaceful in a way that my big empty doublewide isn't.

Sometimes Emily comes down the street to check on me, since school let out. Emily's best friend lived in the trailer behind mine, and they moved away at the end of the school year, so I think she's lonely, too.

She has long black hair, dark skin, and bright black eyes. Most of the time this summer I've left the front door open, with just the screen door closed, because I can't afford to run the air conditioner. She'll ride up on her bike, park it by the porch, and come peer in the screen. Then she'll yell, "Hello? Are you okay in there?" And when I go out to say hi, and tell her I'm fine, really, she'll ask me to read to her. She always has a book or two in her bike basket. So we'll sit on the front porch swing and I'll read, and then she'll smile and pat my shoulder, and tell me everything's going to be okay.

Sometimes I kind of believe her. Sometimes I can convince myself that I'm going to find a great job, and that I like being single.

But then Kim calls to talk, and it's like the divorce is brand new again. I know she's not coming back. She's living with some policeman now. But when she calls to talk, I wonder if she misses me a little. Maybe her life isn't really that great without me. She drinks a lot now, and I worry about her.

It's thoughts like these that make it impossible to sleep all morning. I roll out of bed, put on some cut-offs and a t-shirt, and make a little coffee. Even making one cup at a time, I'll be out by the end of the week. I fill my mug, and go out to sit on the front porch.

Not quite ten yet, and it's already ninety degrees. The sun is about to peek over the top of the house, and the shade is almost gone, but the seat of the porch swing isn't too hot yet. I keep the cordless phone with me just in case somebody calls about a job. Today might be the day.

I've only been sitting here about one minute when George, who lives in the trailer across the street, comes hurrying over. That surprises me, since he's not the type or the size that usually hurries over anything.

He looks a little like Winnie the Pooh, with his chubby, questioning face that always seems a little confused, although there's nothing cute about him. The others in the neighborhood avoid him, probably because he repeats the same boring stories over and over. Or because he never wears a shirt over his big hairy belly. But I don't mind the company.

Today, though, he's hurrying. I sip my coffee and watch him shuffle across the wide asphalt street in his cutoff sweats and worn out rubber flip flops and wonder what's up.

"Did you hear?" he asks, climbing the steps and leaning against the house to catch the last bit of shade.

"What?" My pulse picks up a bit, although I have no idea why, yet.

"The Morenos had a wreck on their way home from the lake." He's still panting a little, as if he just ran a couple of blocks instead of just across the street.

"How did you hear?" It's easy not to believe him, first because I don't want to, but also because the Morenos would never speak to him on the street, much less call him in a disaster. How could he know before me? He must have gotten the news mixed up.

"Tammy was telling the manager about it at the office this morning when I went to pay my rent."

This is bad. It could be real. Tammy is Melody Moreno's best friend in the trailer park, and if anybody knew, it would be her. I squeeze my coffee mug in both hands, still not wanting to believe him. A hot breeze blows by, and it makes me realize that my face is wet with sweat.

"Was anyone hurt?" I ask.

"The little boy broke his leg," he says, and I picture Landon hobbling around on crutches. He's only five, and small for his age. "I guess the little girl was killed, though," George continues, his pudgy face growing long with the news.

I shake my head and feel my stomach churning. It can't be true; in fact, I know it's not possible. Emily was riding her bicycle in front of my house last week, the day they left. She brought over the princess book and we read it on this porch swing while her parents loaded up the camper. There's no way she's gone. "What about Melody and Angel?"

"Here comes Tammy. She knows more about it than me." He points up the street, toward the office, and I see her walking toward us with her head down. She lives in the trailer next to George.

"Tammy!" I yell, and wave when she looks up. She raises a hand part way, but then instead of waving she wipes her face with the neck of her t-shirt. Even from here I can see she's crying.

Tammy is young, just twenty-one, and has been home a lot this summer, too. Her husband Steve is an electrician, and whenever he has lots of work, she quits her job and stays home with her little boy, Dalton. Her mom knows lots of people, and can always get her a job as a receptionist or a filing clerk or whatever when she gets tired of being at home, or when Steve gets off his meds and goes nuts, or whatever.

I want to think of all these things instead of what I know she's coming across the yard to tell us, and I take a drink of my coffee, which is lukewarm now, probably cooler than the air around me. It makes my tongue feel bitter and thick, and doesn't help at all with the lump that's growing in my throat.

"George overheard you talking about Melody and Angel at the office," I say, suddenly wishing she hadn't come over.

"It's true." She sniffs hard and wipes her eyes on her shirt again, then sits down on the porch swing beside me. It rocks me a little, and I plant my feet to steady us.

"What happened?" I ask, when she doesn't go on.

"Angel fell asleep driving, and the camper jack-knifed. All the kids were thrown out." She stops and looks out across the yard. Her voice is even, with no catches or sobs, but tears are streaming down her face.

I set my coffee down on the porch and start rocking the swing back and forth a little, waiting for her to go on, but wishing she wouldn't. She pulls her feet up into the seat of the swing, tucking her knees under her chin, and I notice that her pink fuzzy house slippers are black around the edges from the asphalt and the melted tar.

"The twins are okay?" I prompt.

"Yeah. It's a miracle. They landed in a muddy spot. Hardly even have bruises. And Landon's leg is broken, and two of his ribs."

"What about Melody and Angel?"

"They were wearing their seat belts. They're fine."

I can't ask about Emily, but I think she knows I know, since she doesn't say.

George clears his throat, and I'm startled to remember that he's there. "When will they be back?" he asks. He wipes his eyes with the back of a finger. He's tenderhearted. Most people around here don't know that.

"Tomorrow, probably. Landon and the twins are in the

hospital, getting checked over. Melody's pretty hysterical, still. They'll probably give her some sedatives or something." She sighs and stands up, throwing the porch swing out of rhythm. "I gotta check on Dalton. I'll let you know if I hear anything else."

After she goes home, George stands around for a few more minutes not saying anything, and then shuffles back across the street to his trailer. I just sit here, feeling the sun getting hotter and hotter on my forehead.

It might be a few minutes, or even an hour later, I don't know, when the phone rings. I'd forgotten it was there. After so much time spent wishing it would ring, now I wish it wouldn't. It seems like a violation of the silence. I want to chuck it into the shrubs at the end of the porch. But I answer it anyway, because it might be about a job.

It's Kim on the other end, and I can tell by the way she says "Hey, what's up?" that she's cleaning someone's house. She likes to talk on the phone while she works, but her new boyfriend sleeps during the day. So she calls me. I close my eyes and picture her with the phone tucked between her left ear and shoulder, picking things up with one hand while she dusts under them with the other, then sets them down with a little thump.

She's in the middle of a story about some people she went out and got drunk with over the weekend when I guess she notices that I'm not saying much.

"Um, is something wrong?"

I wonder if I have the strength to tell her. If I say it out loud, I might start to believe it, though. I don't want to believe it. "Melody and Angel had a wreck," I say, thinking I probably won't tell her everything, anyway. She never did care much for Melody and Angel, or anybody else out here. Including me, I guess.

"Are they okay?"

I hear curiosity in her voice, but not concern. I definitely won't tell her. "They are. The kids weren't buckled in, though. They're pretty banged up."

"They had their seatbelts on, but not their kids? That's so stupid! They're just lucky no one was killed."

My eyes start overflowing, and a great pressure in my chest turns into a kind of sob before I can stop it.

"What?" She's heard me, but there's nothing I can do about it now. I've got tears rolling down my cheeks, and I can't catch my breath.

"Emily," I say, and that's all I can get out. I suddenly realize it's for real that she won't be checking in on me anymore, or wanting me to read her favorite book to her.

"Oh, god," Kim says, in kind of a quiet voice. I think she sounds sad, not disgusted with me for crying, but it's hard to tell. She always said I was too emotional. "Is it bad?" she asks.

"Yeah," I manage to gasp.

"Do you want me to come over there when I finish work?"

"No," I say, when I catch my breath. At one time, I would've done anything to have her come over, for any reason. But now it seems kind of pointless. She's moved away from everyone here. I wipe my face on my t-shirt and breathe in and out a few times, pulling myself together. "No. I'm okay. Besides, I don't really know anything yet. The other three kids are still at the hospital. I'll let you know when I hear more."

It isn't until almost dark that evening that anything happens. I'm sitting in my recliner watching re-runs on TV when there's a knock on the screen door. The porch light isn't on because the moths and June bugs get so bad, so I don't see that it's Angel until I open the door. He takes a long drag on his cigarette and grinds it out on the porch railing. In the darkness, his eyes look like black holes.

"Hey, Jason. Can I come in?" His voice is hoarse, there's a big purple bruise on his forehead, and dark brown smears of what's probably blood on his t-shirt and his ragged cut-offs.

"Sure, sure." I open the door wider, and he walks past me into the living room. I turn off the TV as he sits down on the couch, and I sit down in the recliner facing him.

He doesn't say anything for a minute, and I wait, thinking that he's probably not ready to say anything, and if he does I'll probably start crying again, anyway.

"You heard what happened?" He chokes up a little on the question.

I nod, swallowing hard. He didn't come over to watch me cry; I've got to hold it together in case he needs to talk about it. For some reason, everybody in the neighborhood comes to me to talk like I'm some kind of therapist. Probably because I listen.

"I wanted to stop for the night, you know?" He rubs his eyes. "I was so sleepy my eyes wouldn't focus. But Melody said we needed to get home. The kids were all asleep in the back of the van. She wanted to hurry and get home." He covers his face with his hands and moans. "I should've stopped anyway. I can't believe I did this."

"It was an accident," I say, surprised at how strong my voice sounds.

He moans, shakes his head and runs his hands up into his hair, grabbing at it like he's going to tear it out.

"It was an accident," I say again. "It wasn't anybody's fault." I can't believe that completely, since the kids weren't buckled in, but I for sure can't blame him for letting Melody bully him into coming home when he wanted to stop and rest.

He looks up at me, and I've never seen pain so hard across anybody's face before. It hurts me just to meet his eyes, but I do, hoping it'll help.

"I don't remember everything," he says slowly, still looking straight at me. "I guess when it happened, I hit the steering wheel." He stops and runs his fingertips carefully across the long bruise above his eyebrows.

"When I came to, Melody was out in the ditch screaming the kids' names. The van was on its side, and the top of it was gone. I crawled out, and we looked. We found the twins under part of the van roof, but they were okay. Landon was crumpled up a little ways further, but he was breathing good so we kept looking." He stops and takes a few deep breaths, wiping his wet cheeks with the back of his hand.

I have a roll of toilet paper next to the recliner from when I was crying earlier. I give it to him and he pulls off a strip and blows his nose before he goes on. "I think she was still alive when we found her. She was a little warm." He trembles, and seems to get smaller. "Her arm—Melody kept trying to, like, put it back on, or something, screaming to her that she was okay." He shakes his head. "I wanted to do CPR, I was going to try. But her face was so messed up, I couldn't find her mouth. Then it was too late." He puts his face in his hands again, sobbing. "She was cold."

I move over to sit next to him, and when I put my hand on his shoulder, he leans against me.

I've always had a pretty good imagination, and it's going nuts on me now. It's almost like I can feel the panic, smell the blood and the oil and the mud, see poor Emily all torn apart. My head spins with how awful it is, and I want to puke.

He pulls away from me without looking at me, grabs the

toilet paper and wipes up his face. When he finally does look up at me, I know that what I feel is only a tiny sliver of what he feels.

"How can I live with this?" he whispers. "I can't live with this."

I can't imagine living with it, either, but I can't say that. What can I say?

"You were a great dad to Emily," I finally tell him, glad that it's true. Emily was a happy girl, and she loved him, and I tell him that, too. "You still have three boys at home who need you. They're going to have a hard time with this."

He closes his eyes and presses his lips together, like he's trying to pull everything back in, put it back together in his mind. Then he opens his eyes and nods his head. "Yeah. You're right, man. My boys need me." He takes a deep breath, and then lets it out slowly. After a while he stands up. "Thanks, man."

"You going to be okay?" It's a stupid question. Of course he's not. But I don't want him to leave yet if he's going to go home and blow his brains out or something.

He sort of nods, and then stares at the ground like he forgot what to do next.

"Come over any time," I tell him. "I'm always here." I walk out onto the porch with him, and he shakes my hand before he leaves. I hope he'll come back if things get too bad.

For the first time, I'm glad I haven't gotten a job yet, even though I'm almost completely broke and the bills are all coming due in a couple of weeks. Maybe Kim's right and I'm not good for much, but I can listen. It seems like that's pretty important, even to her. After all, she keeps calling.

I remember I told her I'd call her when I heard something about the wreck. I grab the phone and carry it out to the porch swing with me.

Once I'm there, I sit down, put the phone on the seat beside me and look around. Things aren't that dark once my eyes adjust. I can see Tammy's and George's trailers across the street. Neither one has lights on, but they're probably still up watching TV.

Except for those two trailers, that side of the street is empty all the way up to the entrance. There isn't a trailer around mine on this side of the street until Melody and Angel's, four lots down, and then another one way up the street, near the manager's office.

I wonder if Emily is a ghost now, roaming around out here somewhere. I've seen ghosts before, when I cleaned houses. They always seemed sad, though. I hope she's not sad. I hope she can move on to some place where she's happy.

I think about calling Kim, but I don't really want to talk to her. None of this belongs to her anymore. This is my world, not hers.

I sway back and forth a little, leaning back to look up at the stars. It feels like the sky and the ground are moving around me, instead of me being the one who's moving.

Queen of Cups

Beth Wilson/Personal Loans

MONDAYS WERE ALWAYS SLOW DAYS in the classified ads department, since most people call to place their ads at the end of the week for the Sunday paper. As I sat in my cubicle waiting for the phone to ring, and it didn't, I couldn't help thinking about this dream I'd had for the thirteenth time that morning.

In my dream I was morbidly obese. In real life I'm about ten pounds overweight. Not enough that I want to join a gym or anything – just one size bigger than I want to be. But in my dream I sat on a filthy old loveseat, and I took up the whole darn thing. My thighs pressed against the armrests in a way that pinched.

I wore a flowered muumuu dress that was soaked with sweat because it was super hot. My house was a shack, with only the one small room that I sat in. The walls were weathered gray wood and boxy square shelves full of cheap knick-knacks hung in two rows all the way around the room. The dirt floor had piles of straw in the corners.

As I sat there feeling like there was something important I needed to remember, the whole place was suddenly in flames. The straw and the wood went up like kindling, turning black as the flames reached for me and cinders fell in my hair. Smoke burned my throat and my lungs, but I couldn't move without help. I screamed and called for someone named Betty. I always woke up screaming and coughing and choking, full of panic.

Normally the dream was the same every time, but that morning there had been chickens in the house. They had nests in the boxes hanging from the walls. For the first time, I recognized the room as a chicken coop. I'd never seen one before in real life, but it was pretty obvious. Then they disappeared, and I was there on the loveseat, and the rest of the dream was the same. It took me thirty minutes and a cool shower to calm down and stop coughing. I was even upset with Betty, whoever she was. It was that real.

The long shower and the calming down time made me almost late, and I had to wait until I got to work to e-mail my dream to my friend Mavis so she could tell me what she thought it meant. So far her interpretations hadn't been especially helpful, but I was getting desperate to get it figured out so I could stop having the dream. I fiddled around anxiously, waiting for her to e-mail me back.

Mavis was one of my best friends, but she was out there. She belonged to this group that worshiped spirits and held séances and all that. It met every Tuesday, and she'd been trying to get me to go. She said there was a guy who was really good with dreams who could probably help me more than she did. I'd been resisting, but after this time, I decided I'd probably go with her.

I had decided to go once before, not because of the dream but because she was my friend and it meant a lot to her. That time, though, I made the mistake of telling my dad about it, and he made fun of them so much I changed my mind.

My dad was an atheist, but I think he just didn't want the responsibility that went along with believing in a god. He made fun of pretty much every religion and belief system except Catholicism. That was because my mom was a Catholic, and she wouldn't let him. Catholics are about as far as you can get from atheists, though. They have lists of rules and rituals for everything. My mom insisted I attend Catholic school up until high school, but after that my dad insisted I get a public education to balance me out. Between them I ended up with a healthy respect for God with a healthy dose of skepticism for organized religions.

I don't know how my parents managed to get along so well when they were such complete opposites, but they did. And they were always there for me.

After two hours at work, I finally got a call for an ad, and while I was taking care of that, I got an e-mail from Mavis.

"Chickens in a dream symbolize cowardliness and a lack of willpower, Audrey," she wrote. "I've told you before what I think the rest of the dream means - you have low self-esteem, and you need to undergo a transformation in your soul and psyche. Come to a meeting with me. It will help you to change your life."

I was a little bit offended at her interpretation, but the only way to prove her wrong was to go with her. Not that I had to prove her wrong. But still. I e-mailed her back and told her to pick me up at my apartment the next evening, and this time I didn't tell my dad I was going.

Mavis was a completely ordinary-looking person most of the time, with shoulder-length, light brown hair and a narrow face. Her eyes weren't big or small, and her nose was just the slightest bit crooked. But when I got in her car the next evening, she was wearing a vividly purple pompadour wig that rubbed the ceiling of her car and a flowing linen dress in the exact same color of purple.

She reminded me of a character from The Simpsons.

"So, is it okay if I wear jeans and a t-shirt?" I asked as I put on my seatbelt, feeling like I'd like to back out now. But it was too late; she was already pulling away from the apartment. Her little Toyota felt way too small for the two of us and her costume.

"I'm only wearing this because I'm part of the ceremony," she said. "Most of the group will be dressed casual."

"Well, that's a relief. My neighbor borrowed my wig, and I haven't got it back yet," I said. She gave me a sideways look and didn't crack a smile.

"You could really have fun tonight if you let yourself, you know Audrey?" She stopped at the light and turned to look at me. "This is going to be the most enlightening night of your life. You wait and see."

That's when I noticed she had a purple sequin stuck between her eyebrows.

Mavis stopped the car next to the curb behind two other cars on a wide street in front of a house that was bigger than my sorority house in college, but was much newer. There were already four cars in the circle driveway. Who would have thought Mavis's psycho group had money?

"Crap," she muttered. "I was supposed to get here early."

"Sorry," I said, although it wasn't my fault. I had been ready fifteen minutes when she finally showed up at my apartment.

"No big deal." She yanked up on the emergency brake, threw her keys in her bag, and opened the door. "Oh, I almost forgot," she said, turning suddenly to me. "My group name is DayStar." She stared for a couple of seconds, watching my reaction, so I was careful not to let the tiniest grin pop out. It was difficult, though.

When she was satisfied I wasn't going to make fun of her, she put one hand on the top of her purple hair and guided it out of the car door. I got out and followed her up to the house. The landscaping in the yard included a fountain and lots of low shrubs.

As we walked up the steps, the front door was opened by a tall, blond-haired man. My first thought was that he was hot and I wouldn't mind asking him out. But he was a little out of my league. I'm cute, but he looked more like a cologne model.

At least he was wearing jeans and a t-shirt; I felt a little less awkward since he was dressed like a normal person.

"DayStar! Glad you're here. They've already started setting

up in the kitchen."

"This is my friend, Audrey, with the dream," she told him, gesturing at me as she hurried across the entry way – which was bigger than my apartment and decorated with what looked to me like French antiques. "Audrey, this is WindSong."

"You can call me Jeff," he said, winking conspiratorially as he shook my hand.

"What did Mavis tell you about my dream?" I asked. It made me uneasy to think she was blabbing stuff I told her to total strangers.

"She said you had lots of crazy dreams, and I would probably find them interesting." He smiled. "And I would love to hear them, if you want to share."

"You're the guy who interprets dreams?" I was surprised. He looked more like a surfer than a psychic. At least, he didn't look anything like the psychics on info-mercials and daytime talk shows. I had expected, at the very least, flowing robes and long hair. Especially after seeing Mavis's get-up that evening.

"Oh, yeah. And I read cards, too." He pulled a deck of cards a little bigger than playing cards out of his back jeans pocket. "Are you interested in telling me your dream? I'm here by the door to direct traffic, but we could sit down and talk if you don't mind interruptions."

He gestured to a settee with light blue cushions beside the door.

"Sure," I said. We sat down and I told him all about my dream. A couple of times I had to stop while he got the door, but that wasn't nearly as distracting as the fact that he kept shuffling his cards and laying them out in a row, then gathering them up and doing it again.

"Are the cards telling you what my dream means?" I asked, when I finished and he didn't say anything right away.

He looked up at me and grinned. "Nah. I'm only using them to focus my thoughts."

"Oh." I nodded like I knew what he was talking about. "Well, Mavis, I mean, DayStar, or whatever her name is," I paused, trying to get my thoughts back together. "Anyway, she says that my dream means I need to undergo a transformation in my soul, and the chickens mean I don't have the courage to do it."

Jeff shook his head. "Mavis means well, but she gets her interpretations from a dream dictionary on the Internet."

"So that's not a good way to do it?" I couldn't help noticing that his eyes were deep and very dark – almost black.

"Not at all. There are lots of different kinds of dreams. The kind that's just cleaning out your unconscious so you can think clearly the next day, the kind that acts out your phobias and issues to help you deal with them better, the kind that tells the future—" he paused.

"Which one is mine?" I asked, leaning forward anxiously. Not the kind that told the future, I hoped.

"None of them." He started shuffling the cards again. "Your dream is telling you about your past life."

This took a minute to sink in. Naturally I didn't believe in past lives. Maybe my mom was right and you go up or down, heaven or hell – or possibly purgatory. Maybe my dad was right and this was all we had. But either way, you didn't come back. I'd never even considered reincarnation as a rational belief choice.

Then there was the issue of who I was in my dream. How could he think I was that person? I gave him a dirty look. "I have never been a fat woman who lived in a chicken coop!"

"What is it about being that person that bothers you?" he asked calmly, as if this were a normal conversation to be having.

"Poor? Stupid? Ridiculously obese? I'm not any of those things."

"There are lots of good people who have been poor, ignorant, and overweight. Those three things don't make a person bad. Usually they just indicate tough circumstances."

Things must've been pretty tough if I was living in a chicken coop. Not that I believed him. "It was just a dream," I insisted. "That's all it was. I don't even believe in reincarnation."

He shrugged his shoulders, looking completely nonchalant. "You don't have to believe in something for it to be true."

"Well," I said, but then I stopped. I had just said that to my dad the week before when we were arguing about the existence of God. Dang it. "What makes you think it was the fourth kind of dream, anyway?"

"It's just a feeling I have." He smiled and shrugged almost apologetically.

"Ah." It had been stupid of me to get my hopes up that he could help me with the dream. He didn't know any more than Mavis did, with her purple hair and her Internet dictionary. I needed a therapist, not a psychic.

"You're skeptical about all this." He looked up from the cards straight into my eyes.

I probably would have said "duh" if he weren't so cute. Instead I just nodded.

"It's okay," he said. "I understand."

And he looked so understanding and so kind with his big, dark eyes that I wished I believed him. Even though he was being ridiculous.

"These cards are a guide," he said, fanning them out so I could see the artwork on them. "I look at them and see symbols that help me interpret my feelings, but it's the feeling I have that's right. I'm rarely wrong when I sense something this strongly."

I wished I had brought my own car so I could leave. I felt let down, and my stomach felt twisty and upset. There was no reason to let any of this bother me; it was a joke. Still, it mattered.

"Look, your dream isn't a bad thing," he said. "Just because you were somebody with fewer resources in a past life."

"Fewer resources?" Was he making fun of me?

"No, really. Listen. Say I told you in your last life you were a queen. Would that make you feel better?"

I shrugged and nodded. "Yeah. I guess."

"You wouldn't wonder even a little bit what you did wrong that you weren't royalty this time around?"

"Huh." He had a point. Darn him.

"You had a hard life last time, but, just judging from your appearance, you look like you're doing okay this time."

I nodded, relaxing a little. "My life is pretty good," I admitted.

"Regardless of your difficult circumstances, you must have had a good heart." He started shuffling the cards again. "You had a hard life. Your physical and mental limitations kept you from doing much. Basically, they kept you from surviving. In the end, you were trapped by them."

I remembered being unable to move in my dream, and that suffocating feeling, and I felt a little panicky, which seriously annoyed me. "And that's no big deal because--?"

"Oh, I never said it was no big deal," he said, looking up at me. "It seems like a pretty big deal to me, actually. I can imagine you're very concerned by the whole thing. What I said was, your dream isn't a bad thing. What you need to ask yourself, is why you keep having it."

"That's what I came here to ask you."

"Is that what you asked me?"

I had thought it was, but now I was confused. I hated it when people answered questions with questions. "I thought you could interpret my dream and I could get past it," I said. "I don't want to have this dream anymore."

He nodded and shuffled his cards again. "You came because you wanted answers." He laid out three cards and looked at them, then picked up the middle card and flipped it around so I could see it. "Queen of Cups." He smiled as if that was some kind of answer.

I took the card and studied the picture. It had a woman on a giant shell throne on a beach, and she was holding a silver cup covered with a veil. It meant absolutely nothing to me. "Is this supposed to be an answer?" I asked.

He nodded. "The cup is a symbol for the emotional world, if that helps. But honestly, you can find the answers without cards or symbols. They're in your heart. You have a good heart." He took the card from my hand and shuffled it into the deck, and then he put the whole deck in his back jeans pocket. "I've got to get to the kitchen. It's time for the ceremony."

"I think I'll just wait in here," I said. I had no desire to watch Mavis and her friends dance around in colored wigs and robes. The whole point of coming was to find out what my dream meant so I would stop having it, not to participate in some stupid ritual. If I wanted to do that, I could've gone to mass with my mom.

"If you change your mind, the kitchen is through that doorway, all the way down the hall to the last door on your left. But you'll hear the music." He smiled at me, and then left.

I sighed, feeling frustrated. It looked like I was going to have to figure this out on my own. I closed my eyes and leaned my head back, reliving what Jeff had said were the last few moments of my last life.

It didn't take long to recall the chicken coop, the loveseat, and the dirt floor. The sensory details were just as real as when I was asleep. I saw the flames start this time. The single lightbulb hanging from the ceiling by a wire shorted out. The sparks flew from the ceiling in slow motion, catching on the straw on the floor and in the boxes right away, and then grabbing the wood. The heat was intense, and my eyes and throat stung with the smoke. I felt the weight of my body, but was completely powerless to move. I covered my nose and mouth with the collar of my dress so I could breathe as I screamed for Betty, squinting to see through the smoke to the door.

When I realized it was too late for Betty to help even if she did come, I felt sad for her. I hoped she wouldn't be the one to find me, and that she knew how much I appreciated her taking care of me. I leaned back and closed my eyes and stopped fighting. It was time to give up.

I opened my eyes and felt disoriented to see the huge room around me. It took a few seconds to adjust to being Audrey again. Maybe reincarnation wasn't that far-fetched. The other me had been different, but still me. It had been so real.

Jeff had said I had a good heart; I thought maybe he was right. He was right about my life now, too. It was a good life, and I was enjoying it.

So maybe he was right about the rest. But if so, what did that mean? If I'd gotten from there to here by having a good heart, where could I go from here with all the resources I had now?

A drumbeat started, and I heard people laughing and talking. I wondered what Mavis's part in the ceremony would entail. I couldn't help being a little bit curious what would require such a crazy costume.

I stood up and followed the sound down the hall. After all, I had told Mavis I'd try it out, and sulking in the other room didn't count.

It seemed like a good time to join the party.

The Essential Johnny Cash

WHEN MICHAEL WAS SIX YEARS OLD his favorite singer was Johnny Cash, and his favorite song was "Sunday Morning Coming Down." He had this song on a 45 LP, and he played it over and over at top volume until his mother would scream at him to "turn that thing off, for god's sake!" It was a depressing song, really, about an alcoholic wandering the empty sidewalks on Sunday morning feeling sorry for himself. Not at all appropriate for a six-year-old.

That was the same year that his family lived in a farmhouse by the railroad tracks on the west side of Enid, in Northern Oklahoma. It was a genuine farmhouse with five acres, two separate horse pastures, a barn, and a chicken coop. Michael had his own pony, but it wasn't broken, so he couldn't ride it. He liked playing with the chickens, though. They had thirty. And there was a pig, several dogs, and a tiger cat that scratched anyone who tried to pet him. They also had two descented skunks living in the house as pets. Someone told his mom they ate roaches.

The family moved quite a few times during Michael's elementary school years, but he was just now in first grade and not aware of the difficulties of going from school to school. There were other difficulties he was aware of.

For example, his mom had a boyfriend or two by this time, men introduced to Michael as Uncle Charlie or Uncle Frank who came over to their house during the evening while his dad was at work. The one she was seeing when they lived at the farmhouse the year he was six was Uncle Billy.

Pattie, Michael's mom, was tall and very thin at that time, with bleached blonde hair, fair skin, and very pale blue eyes. Michael thought she was beautiful when she was being nice. She worked as a waitress in the local drugstore cafe. Billy was a mechanic who had a shop nearby. He was a regular customer at the café, which is how they took up with each other.

Michael's dad, Robert, worked for Failings, a local oil rig building company named after the owner. Robert worked in assembly for years and then became a foreman. He was eventually fired because Pattie would call and threaten the women who worked with him. She developed an unhealthy paranoia from her own escapades and the diet pills she took to stay thin.

But that was later. At the time when Michael was starting

first grade his dad was doing well at work, bringing home some money. They had two nice cars and three junkers, and a big screen TV that came in a big shiny wooden cabinet and took up one whole wall in the living room. Robert fixed his black hair in a shiny wave high over his forehead like Johnny Cash, and his dark eyes were focused and bright. His hands were always rough with black in the creases and under the nails. He worked on the junker cars to relax.

Michael also had an older sister, Susan, who was twelve. Susan was born when Pattie was just sixteen and Robert was twenty-two. That was back in the days before people thought about high school girls dating men several years older as being improper. It was still more natural for girls to get married and have kids than to go to college. At least, that's the way it was in Enid.

A few years after Susan came Robbie, who was just a year-and-a-half older than Michael, and was his mom's favorite. Robbie would come up and put his head on his mom's lap when she was watching TV and say, "Rub my head, Mama." And she would sit there and rub her hands through his hair like he was a puppy or a kitten.

Last of all came Michael himself, completely by accident.

When he started first grade, Michael hadn't yet learned that you have to be a bully or get bullied. He was still innocent in some things, even though he knew all about hiding in his bedroom listening to "Sunday Morning Coming Down" so loud that he couldn't hear his parents screaming at each other. There were crashes a lot of times too. Things got broken. But he stayed in the bedroom he shared with Robbie, who didn't like his choice of songs and complained plenty.

Afterward his dad went to work, Susan went to a friend's house, and Billy would come over. Pattie would scream "turn that gawdawful song off, for god's sake!" And then things would be quiet for a while. He and Robbie could go in the living room and watch TV all night if they wanted, as long as they kept the volume down low.

Pattie mostly worked weekends, and then a couple of days during the week. Michael liked weekends, because he could hang out with his dad without his mom getting mad and throwing things. Usually his dad was working on an old car, and Michael and Robbie would go and fetch tools for him when he asked for them. Then they played nearby and kept an eye out for the tools to come flying back out from underneath the car, Robert cussing up a storm for whatever went wrong.

One Saturday, about lunchtime, Michael looked up from his cars (he was denting them with a piece of brick so they would look wrecked) and saw his dad, wearing a clean shirt, coming out of the front door of the house.

"You want to come with me to the post office?" Robert asked.

Naturally Michael did. Anytime he got to do something with just his dad, it made him feel special. Plus, when everybody wasn't going somewhere, his dad would drive the Shelby Mustang, which was the coolest sportscar they'd ever had.

Robert drove to the post office, parked on the street, and went in. Michael stayed in the car with the windows rolled down, staring at how the heat made the baking sidewalk look wavy and interesting, instead of just dirty and hot. He wiped the sweat off his forehead; it felt gritty and slimy because Robbie had dumped dirt in his hair earlier, and he hadn't washed afterward, but just ran his fingers through his hair to shake it out.

Both boys got their hair buzzed off into crew cuts at the beginning of every summer, but by the time school started up, they both had curls around their ears and on their necks again. Summer in Oklahoma usually lasted till about the middle of October, although it stopped being quite so hot after the middle of September or so. Since it was only the first part of September, it was still plenty hot enough for wavy sidewalks on that Saturday.

When Robert came out of the post office, he had a handful of mail in one hand, and a brown package in the other. He tossed it at Michael when he got in the car.

"That's for you," he said.

The package was square, about two inches thick, and five or six inches long. Michael couldn't read yet, so he couldn't tell where it came from. The idea of getting a package was such a surprise, it took him a few seconds to think of opening it. Once he did, though, he ripped through the paper and the cardboard in no time.

It was an eight-track tape of Johnny Cash, with a close-up of his face on the front, leaning back with his eyes closed as he crooned into a microphone, his black hair in a big shiny pouf over his forehead.

"Wow! Is this for me?" Michael asked.

"I figured you needed a new one to listen to," his dad grunted in a way that said he didn't really want a hug, so don't get too excited.

"Wow. Cool. Can we listen to it now?"

Robert put it in the player, but they were already pulling up to the drugstore where Pattie worked.

"Can I stay in the car and listen to it?" Michael asked. He would normally want to go in and see his mom, since she was a lot nicer at work than she was at home, and he usually got a can of soda and sometimes some candy for free.

"I guess," his dad said, kind of smiling now. He left the key turned in the ignition so that the player would stay on.

It was still hot, but now Michael was in the shade of the drugstore. With the windows rolled down and the music playing, it seemed a lot cooler. He sat back in his seat and stared at the window of the drugstore, which was brightly painted with colorful words he couldn't read yet. The inside of the store was dimmer than outside. The people moving around looked like shadows, dim and without any specific color. He turned the music up a little louder.

The first song wasn't even over when he heard yelling from inside the store. He leaned forward to turn the music down, feeling a tightness in his stomach that he wasn't old enough yet to recognize as anxiety, mixed with the tiniest bit of excitement. He stared hard at the glass front door of the store in anticipation.

Almost immediately the shadows of people in the store became real people up near the glass. Then the front door crashed open, and the back of a man was staggering toward him, with his dad coming right behind. His mom stood in the doorway twisting a dishrag between her hands, her lips pressed tight together in a small line.

Then the backwards man caught his balance, but it was too late because Robert had him by the shirt and was punching his nose. It wasn't like the fights in the cowboy shows. There were no loud smacking, popping sounds when his dad hit the man. There was lots of grunting, though, and some yelling that didn't sound like words.

The other man didn't seem to be putting up much of a fight, even though he was a little bit taller than Robert. Then he half turned, like he was trying to get away, and Michael saw it was Billy. So that's why his mom was looking worried, but not saying anything. Michael looked back at her, almost involuntarily, but now she didn't look worried. She had the teeniest bit of a smile on one side of her mouth and she was leaning forward, like she was watching a football game.

Michael looked back at his dad, but already the fight was over. Billy was half scrambling and shuffling down the sidewalk, leaving little drips of blood from his nose on the pavement.

Robert turned around and said something quiet to Pattie, and then he came back to the car. Pattie nodded, her face looking blank now, and went back in the store.

Robert got in the car and started it, the engine roaring to life and temporarily interrupting the music.

"You whupped his butt, Dad," Michael said, excited and a little bit awestruck.

Robert looked down at Michael and smiled. "Yup." His hand was bleeding a little bit, but Billy hadn't hit him even once. He turned the music up a little more. "So. You like this?" He nodded his head toward the radio.

Michael looked down, disoriented. He'd been so absorbed by the fight for the few seconds it had lasted, he'd forgotten about the music. "It's great!" he said, recovering quickly. He had no idea what Johnny was singing about, but the music was lively now, and twangy, and made him want to bounce in his seat.

Trying to Hang On

WHEN MICHAEL WAS TEN YEARS OLD he went with his family to the house of their good friend Larry for New Year's Eve. It was the end of 1976, and life was going well for Michael. He had figured out how to get along with his older brother and sister, he was popular in school, and he even had a girlfriend. His life was finally making sense.

It was a three hour drive to Larry's house, but Michael's family made the trip at least once a month. Michael rode in the middle of the back seat between his sister Susan, who was sixteen, and his brother Robbie, who was twelve.

Susan was already pregnant, but she hadn't told anyone yet. She didn't want to be so much like her mother, who had dropped out of high school to have her, but she'd had an abortion a few months ago and didn't think she wanted another.

Her boyfriend never went with them to Larry's house. He was going to a New Year's Eve party with some friends from school. She'd wanted to go with him and was sulky. Her mood didn't bother Michael, though. He knew that as long as he was quiet and kept to himself, he could get along with her just fine.

It wasn't as easy with Robbie, who thought it was funny to pull Michael's hair and pinch him whenever he started falling asleep. Michael knew better than to complain to his parents, though. If he said anything, he was likely to get slapped at for whining. Instead he did his best to stay awake and keep a good six or eight inches between his skinny shoulders and Robbie's. Every once in a while he got out his hair brush and ran it through his hair, which was chin length and feathered nicely.

Michael had recently discovered personal hygiene. He'd raised his hand in class earlier in the year and noticed that his whole arm was black with dirt. That's when he decided he was going to shower every day. When he told Pattie – his mom – she wrinkled her nose at him and said, "I guess you can if you want to." Since then, she'd made comments about him being "prissy." He didn't feel like the time he spent grooming himself was excessive, though. After all, it was only after he started showering that he had become more popular at school.

But in general, the idea of cleanliness was new to him, and hadn't extended to his environment yet. At ten, he still didn't realize that not everyone had roaches in their houses. He was used to blowing out a bowl or cup before he used it to make sure there were no dead bugs in it, and he assumed that's how it was anywhere.

The old bungalow Larry lived in couldn't help with any future revelations, either. In fact, after visiting Larry's house Michael's home seemed well kept, even though the red shag carpet in their living room had started looking a bit like a dirt floor with red yarn growing out of it.

Michael had noticed by this time that Larry didn't smell clean, and his shoulder length hair was greasy and uncombed. Robbie also had some odor issues, but Michael knew better than to say anything about it. At least this evening Robbie was wearing the cologne he got for Christmas, so the trip hadn't been bad.

When they got to Larry's, quite a few of their friends were already there. Robert – Michael's dad – parked the car along the curb opposite the house and they all got out and hurried across the street. Michael could feel the cold soaking into his lightweight blue and white velour jacket, which he was wearing over his three button pullover with the giant collar and bell-bottomed blue jeans. He also wore Gass shoes, which made him nearly two inches taller. This was his standard outfit regardless of the weather, and he felt stylish and confident in it. He strutted a little as he climbed up the wide front steps of the big porch.

Tom opened the door before they got to it. He was Susan's age, and worked with Larry at the newspaper office in circulation. They put together all the inserts of the paper and got the papers ready for the routes and the mail.

It seemed to Michael that Tom lived at Larry's, since he was there every time they were. Tom did spend more time with Larry than at home, but technically, he still lived with his mom and her fourth husband. Since Larry's mom moved into the nursing home, Tom usually spent the night in her room.

"Come in," he said, giving a hopeful smile to Susan.

Even though she generally had a boyfriend in Enid, in the past she'd allowed Tom boyfriend privileges when she was in Elk City. The last few visits – since she'd been sleeping with Bruce – she kept to herself and snubbed him. Bruce was different than her other boyfriends; she thought she might really be in love with him. Especially now that she was considering having his baby.

Michael felt a little sorry for Tom when he saw Susan turn up her nose and refuse to greet him. He knew what it was like to have a crush who snubbed him, and besides, Michael adored Susan.

Larry had a bar set up on the sideboard in the dining room, which was adjacent to the living room through accordion pleated sliding doors in a double wide doorway. This was where they all headed first. The bar was stacked with bottles of various sizes and shapes and lots of thick yellow glass tumblers, with a cooler full of ice and a keg of beer next to it on the floor.

"Hi!" Larry greeted them enthusiastically, shaking Robert's hand and giving Pattie a half hug. "Good to see you! What'll you have?"

Robert wanted Scotch, Pattie wanted a Vodka tonic, and Susan took a beer. Robbie and Michael knew that if they wanted something with alcohol in it, they only had to wait until no one was looking. Michael's favorite was spiced rum in Pepsi, and Robbie drank whatever Michael made for him.

"Can I be the bartender?" Michael asked Larry.

"Sure!" Larry laughed. "You know how to mix drinks?"

"If people tell me what they want I can do it," he said confidently.

Larry laughed again, his dad shrugged, and the grownups moved away, talking about whatever it is that grownups talk about at parties like that.

Michael pulled up a barstool and settled in. Robbie looked from Michael to the rest of the room, where other people are milling around, and then finally headed over to a nearby coffee table where Tom and a couple of his friends were playing Monopoly, leaving Michael on his barstool by the drinks.

One thing Michael especially liked about his position at the bar was its distance from the basement door, which was in the hallway just off the other side of the living room. Several times he'd been at Larry's when that door had jumped and rattled away on its hinges as if there were some giant on the other side trying to escape. A couple of times, spending the night, Michael heard moans along with the rattling. Larry insisted it was the ghost of his dad and no trick.

Whenever it happened, it sparked ghost stories from Michael's dad, the details of which changed to fit the mood and tended to get gorier and more dramatic with each telling. Robert loved a good story, and whether or not it was strictly true had never been relevant to him. As Michael got older, he often wondered if Robert could even tell his facts from fictions.

In spite of the changing stories, Michael believed in the ghost—mainly because he saw the way Larry acted when it happened. Underneath his shaggy beard Larry's face always looked a little green afterward. Kind of like Robbie's did that time after he ate the ham that had been out on the counter for too long.

Michael waited until his parents were on the other side of the room before adding rum to the tumbler of Pepsi he poured for himself. Before he could take a drink Robbie was by his side.

"Gimme that one," he demanded, and Michael handed it over without complaint and started making another. Life was easier if he pretended he was already planning to do whatever Robbie had most recently demanded.

"D'you think the ghost will come out tonight?" Michael asked, sipping his drink and relaxing.

Robbie shrugged, glancing over at the group of grownups each time he took a drink. He was more worried about getting caught with his drink than he was about a ghost. In fact, as paranoid as Robbie got when he was drinking, Michael wondered why he even bothered. To Michael, drinking was like his feathered hair and his wide-collared shirt. It made him feel cool and confident. A chick-magnet. Sort of like Burt Reynolds, his favorite actor. Besides, it tasted good. Ironically, ten years later, it was Robbie who became the alcoholic, while Michael remained a social drinker. By that time he'd discovered other ways to be cool.

Robbie went back to the game with the older boys, and Michael sat and watched the party contentedly. Quite a few of his parents' friends engaged him in conversation as he got their drinks, and he enjoyed being treated like a grownup. He kept the Pepsi can next to his glass in case anyone wondered what he was drinking, but nobody did.

Susan came over and pulled up a barstool at eleven-thirty or so.

"Hey, kid."

"What'll you have?" Michael asked.

"Another beer, I guess."

He pumped the keg, held her beer mug up to the nozzle, and flipped the top, tilting the glass to keep the foam down. His dad showed him how to do this last summer, and now he thought it was even more fun than mixing the drinks. He handed her the glass and returned to his stool.

"Thanks." She took a drink and looked over at him fondly.

"Wanna go shopping this weekend?" he asked her hopefully. She took him shopping once before and asked what he thought about the things she tried on. She even bought two blouses that he recommended. He felt pleased every time she wore either of them now, as if he had bought them for her himself.

"I have to work at the bowling alley," she said. She had a couple of part time jobs after school, which cut into her time with Bruce but kept her out of her mom's way. They also gave her alibis when she needed them. "Maybe we could go after I get paid next Tuesday." She was thinking that if she kept the baby, she'd need to buy some dresses to hide her belly for a while.

She was surprised to discover that she might want to keep the baby. It would get complicated when her mom found out, though. They had a hate/hate relationship.

Pattie took diet pills for years, and sometimes, for no reason anyone could tell, she'd attack Susan and beat her up. Robbie never got much more than a slap, since he was her favorite. Michael frequently got hit with whatever she had in her hand at the moment she got angry with him, and she was frequently angry with him. But it seemed like she was always furious with Susan. Of the three siblings, she got the worst of the violence.

Pattie attacked Robert even more than she did Susan, but he fought back. And sometimes he started it.

It was after three o'clock before people started leaving. Michael had long ago abandoned his position as bartender in favor of a game of Monopoly with Robbie, who had since gone to sleep on one end of the couch. Michael's own head was nodding, but then he saw Larry get out a Ouija board, and he perked back up, joining the grownups at the dining room table. Of all the guests, only Michael's family and Tom were left.

Michael knew about Ouija boards, since he'd seen numerous horror movies at the drive-in with his family. He didn't start going to church until junior high, so he didn't know yet that such things were taboo. He just knew that he got a delicious thrill of terror zinging along his spine when he saw it. He studied the faces of the grownups around the table.

Tom was sitting beside Michael looking at Susan even more wistfully now that he was drunk; she moved away any time he approached. She was standing on the opposite side of the table from them behind the row of chairs on that side, her arms folded across her chest.

Robert was in the belligerent stage of drunkenness, announcing that he'd never been afraid of ghosts. Michael noticed that he didn't question whether there was a ghost, though.

Pattie's face had become hard, her eyes unfocused and her mouth pressed into a firm line. When Michael saw that look at home he hid in his room, but here he felt relatively safe.

Larry had become wistful and teary-eyed, insisting that he would finally talk to his dad and find out why he had haunted the basement for the past sixteen years. He stood at the end of the table in front of the board breathing deeply for a few seconds before placing his hands on the pointer and closing his eyes.

"Daddy? Are you here?" he called out.

Michael glanced nervously toward the basement door.

"Daddy, it's me. It's your son Larry," he went on, his voice wavering unsteadily. "I need to talk to you."

In spite of their various states of drunkenness, everyone in the room had become silent and alert.

Larry fell silent, too, although tears still trickled down his cheeks into his beard. Michael had glanced over at Susan to see what she was thinking when his mom gasped, and his attention was drawn back to the board. Larry's hands moved now, either pushing or following the pointer. His eyes were opened wide, bugging out of his head just a little.

"Daddy?" he asked again.

The pointer moved to "Yes."

He dissolved into incoherent blubbering.

"Pull yourself together and ask him a question!" Robert demanded in a low growl. For all his blustering, he was clenching his fists so that the knuckles were white.

Larry sniffed a couple of times, wiped his cheeks on his shoulders without taking his hands from the pointer, and sighed. "Okay," he said. "Okay. Daddy. I need to know why you're haunting me. What do you want?"

For several seconds, nothing happened. Michael found himself holding his breath in the total silence around him. He glanced around the room and saw everyone leaning forward in anticipation. Then, Larry's hands suddenly twitched and jerked on the pointer like it was being pulled away from him and he was trying to hang on. He gave a little shout, and then flew backward away from the table so hard that his head hit the wall several feet behind him.

Susan screamed, and then the basement door began to shake, jumping around in its frame until it seemed inevitable that it would burst open.

Michael felt his heart beating in his throat, and he could barely breathe. The lights flickered, and he covered his head with his arms, closing his eyes tight. He heard several people cursing and shouting and then the rattling slowed and stopped.

Michael peeked out from under his arms, afraid of what he would see, but afraid not to look.

Robert and Tom were helping Larry to his feet. Pattie and Susan had moved much closer to each other, looking pale and shaken but a little excited, too. Robbie was still asleep on the couch.

Michael got up from the table and went over to Susan, taking her hand and pulling her arm around his shoulders, immediately feeling safer. Any minute now his dad would start telling stories.

"I don't guess you'll be getting any answers from him tonight," Robert said to Larry gruffly. "Might as well put that thing away."

Larry nodded dumbly, but he didn't go near the board. He glanced at it and then took a deep breath and blew it out, looking frightened.

Michael was disappointed in his dad's reaction. He wanted Robert to tell stories and make light of the incident until he knew that it was okay to go to sleep. He was nervous about spending what was left of the night there in the living room so close to the door.

Larry headed off to his room without another word, still looking pale and dazed, like the victim of a natural disaster. Michael's parents went to Larry's mom's old room for the night. Susan curled up on the end of the couch opposite Robbie, and Tom and Michael settled on recliners.

In spite of his fear, he managed to fall asleep in the recliner listening to the soothing sounds of the others breathing.

He woke the next morning with a head that felt like it was full of fuzz. The alcohol, the fright, and the five hours of sleep he ended up with were a bad combination. He groaned and rubbed his eyes, wanting to go back to sleep, but his mom was banging around in the kitchen making breakfast. The pills she took to be skinny made it hard for her to sleep more than three or four hours a night, and she was already full of a jittery energy that made her crash the pans around on the stove, even though she wasn't angry yet.

His dad staggered through the living room on his way to the kitchen in his jeans and undershirt looking rumpled and puffy, rubbing his eyes. Michael heard him growling, and then more crashing of pans as Pattie answered sharply, and then louder crashes as they started yelling, but maybe not quite as loudly as they would have yelled at home.

Then, even though Michael was trying to be asleep and not hear, he could tell that his parents were shoving at each other, knocking each other against the table and chairs and cabinet doors and swearing. He opened one eye to peek around the room and saw that Susan was awake, staring straight ahead of her, and Robbie had his eyes closed so tightly that he couldn't possibly be asleep. Tom, however, seemed to still be genuinely asleep, oblivious to the full-fledged fight going on in the kitchen now.

Robert suddenly slammed through the kitchen door, stomping through the dining room and living room and out the front door into the freezing cold in his sleeveless undershirt. Pattie was still banging pans around in the kitchen, so Michael couldn't tell which one of them won. Maybe nobody did. He opened both eyes and glanced over at Susan. She was still staring straight ahead, both eyes wide.

"You okay?" he asked her, his voice coming out thin and whispery.

She blinked and looked at him for a moment before answering. "Sure. You?"

He nodded and stretched. If she was calm things were probably okay. "I got a hangover, though," he said conspiratorially.

"You do not," she said dismissively. "You barely drank anything. And you shouldn't be drinking, for god's sake. You're just a baby."

"I am not a baby!" he said, sitting up in his chair.

"You're right," she said sarcastically. "You're a big kid now, aren't you."

"Shut up!"

Robbie opened his eyes. "You shut up," he commanded. "I was trying to sleep."

"Why? You fell asleep at nine-thirty last night," Michael said, hoping to get Susan to join him in taunting Robbie so they wouldn't gang up on him. "You shouldn't be tired."

"It was after two o'clock," Robbie said.

"Well, you missed seeing the ghost, anyway." Michael was

smug. For once he had the upper hand with Robbie, and he wasn't going to waste it.

"Huh, uh. You're lying."

"You did miss it," he insisted. "Didn't he, Susan."

"You missed it," she agreed.

"Aw, piss."

Michael couldn't keep from grinning.

"What are you smiling about?" Robbie asked crossly. "Dale Bennet."

"That's not my name," Michael said, the smile sliding from his face.

"It was the name on your tag when we found you in the garbage," Susan said. This was her part of the story. She and Robbie never brought it up unless they were together, as if each of them were only allowed to do one part. "Mom and Dad felt sorry for you and adopted you."

"That's stupid." He knew it wasn't true. Once he had even asked his mom if he was adopted. She'd said, "No. We never would have had another one on purpose." It didn't matter, really, whether it was true. What mattered was that they ganged up on him this way, two bigs against one little. It mattered that he didn't belong.

"Dale Bennet," Robbie said again.

Michael frowned. There was no reason for him to put up with this. He got up and stomped to the front door to find his dad.

The second he stepped out onto the porch he felt better. It was plenty cold out, but the air was clear and thin and the sun was shining. Suddenly everything that happened inside – the party, the ghost, the fight, the teasing – seemed to have happened in a dream.

Robert was sitting in the car, smoking. Michael went around to the passenger side, opened the door, and slid in next to him. His dad glanced over at him, then stared forward again, not really looking out the windshield but just off into space. Michael took this as acceptance and settled in, breathing in the smoke and wondering if he'd be pushing his luck to ask for a cigarette. He decided against it. He and Robbie had been getting cigarettes from the vending machine at the golf course for a while now, and he could inhale smoothly without coughing. That would probably make his dad suspicious.

Instead, he rolled his window down about two inches, just like his dad's, and propped his elbow up on the door handle, just like his dad's. For a minute, he considered asking about the ghost, but it didn't seem as important now.

Robert glanced over at him, and one corner of his mouth went up just a little bit. "What's going on in there?" he asked, tilting his head slightly toward the house. He didn't sound as if he cared much. Just making conversation.

"Was I adopted?" Michael asked.

His dad gave him a good stare, for so long that Michael felt uncomfortable. Then Robert reached over and ruffled his hair. "Look at yourself in the mirror sometime," he said. "You're definitely mine."

Michael thought about this and realized it was true. They both had a round chin, straight pointy nose, and big gray eyes. Michael had blond hair and freckles instead of his dad's darkly tanned skin and black hair, but the features were all the same. He wondered why he'd never noticed it before.

They sat in silence for a minute more, until his dad flicked the cigarette butt out the window. "I reckon breakfast is about ready. What do you think?"

Michael nodded, and they both got out of the car. Following his dad back across the street, Michael wondered if his mom was fixing eggs and bacon, or pancakes. He hoped there were pancakes.

And that Larry had orange juice.

Beth Wilson/Personal Loans

East of Enid

WHEN MICHAEL TURNED SIXTEEN, his dad let him pick his first car from the collection of junkers in the backyard. He chose a rusty, forest green Jeep Willys with wood-grained side panels and no seats in the back. It took a lot of work to keep it running, but it was great for getting around Enid. Enid was the biggest town in North Central Oklahoma, but it still wasn't a very big town.

He needed a car for transportation to and from his job at TG&Y in the electronics department. It paid $3.35 an hour, which was minimum wage that year, but the discounts he gave himself and his friends on merchandise made it well worth his time.

He also needed a car because his girlfriend of eighteen months, Tina, felt that it was time to consummate their relationship. Tina's parents never left them alone for a second at their house. Michael's parents didn't care what he did as long as he didn't bother them, but there were too damn many people in his house. And so, the Jeep became both vehicle and location in the fulfillment of that goal, especially over the summer months.

Transportation was freedom to work and to pursue his relationship, but it was also freedom from his family. Michael was the youngest, and nobody's favorite. He was just an accident they couldn't really afford, and he knew that because his mom had told him so plenty of times.

One evening – it was several months later, during Christmas break – when Tina was supposed to be in bed already, her dad caught her sneaking out the window and saw Michael's Jeep at the curb. There wasn't another rusty, forest green Jeep Willys with wood-grained side panels in Enid, so it was no good pretending it was someone else. He'd never felt like Michael was good enough for Tina, but this gave him a reason to actively dislike him. Tina was forbidden to go out with Michael again.

Naturally, this didn't stop them from being together at school, and any time outside of school that Tina could come up with an alibi. That wasn't enough for Michael and Tina, though, and it only took about a month of sneaking around before she came up with a solution.

Her brilliant solution occurred to her during HomeEc, when Michael was at the VoTech learning small engine repair. She had to wait until three to see him again.

During that time she was able to refine her idea and work out the details, so that when they finally met by his locker, she was jumping up and down with excitement and about ready to drag him away from the school.

"Hurry up and get your stuff! I have something important to tell you!" she said, pulling on his arm.

It was obviously good news, so he grabbed his homework and his jacket and followed her out to the bleachers by the football field. There was no one out there since it was cool and drizzly, and the bleachers were soaked. Instead of sitting on them she dragged him around underneath and perched on the crossbars between the support posts.

"So, you know how my dad's being a total prick," she said.

"What did he do now?" Michael asked, preparing himself to get upset.

"Nothing new," she said. "But I'm just sick of having to sneak around to be with you. I mean, I love you and you love me. Why can't he accept that, right?"

"Right," Michael agreed. He was an affectionate boy, and it always made him feel good when she talked about love so matter-of-factly.

"We're planning to get married someday, right?"

He nodded. They'd talked about it before, and he planned to propose as soon as they graduated. He hadn't saved any money for a ring yet, but they had more than a year left of school, so he figured he had time.

"What if," she said dramatically, holding her hands up by her face and bouncing a little, "we got married now?"

Michael wasn't following her. "We aren't old enough. You have to be eighteen."

"Unless you have your parents' consent," she added.

"We don't have that." He frowned. "Your dad hates me. Why would he let us get married?" The answer to that popped into his head before he was completely done asking the question, but he rejected it as too crazy. Until she said it out loud.

"He'd let us get married if I was pregnant." She wrapped her arms around herself and spun triumphantly. "He'd have to."

"Wow," Michael said. He was so surprised she was considering it that he wasn't sure how to react.

"See what I mean?" she said, nodding as if he had just told her the plan was brilliant.

"How would we support ourselves, though?" he asked.

She was ready for this question. "You have a job," she said. "I'll get one, too. We can get some cheap little place and save up for when the baby's born. That won't be for almost a year and by then we'll be almost done with school, anyway. You can work full time after that, and I can stay home with the baby so we won't have to pay for daycare."

Her mom had never worked or even had a driver's license, so this plan seemed logical to Tina. Both of Michael's parents had always worked, but he thought if he could make enough money there was no need for Tina to leave the baby with someone else so she could wait tables. As he thought that through he realized he was accepting her plan, and he really liked the idea.

He wanted to be an adult more than anything. He was sick of his parents beating the shit out of each other and anybody who got in their way. He was sick of his brother breaking his stuff, and he was sick of babysitting his sister's kids for free so she could hang out at the bowling alley and drink. He knew he could do better than any of them, and he was ready to prove it.

They had never had sex without protection before, and they didn't know how long it took to get pregnant. It was harder for them to find a time and place since her parents were being so vigilant in keeping tabs on her at all times. The first month came and went without success, surprising both of them. As many of their classmates got pregnant by accident, they figured it would happen immediately.

The second month, though, Tina dragged Michael out to the bleachers again to tell him she was late. After that, he met her by her locker every morning and found her smiling and giving him the thumbs up. A couple of weeks later, she reported a faint sense of nausea coming over her at random moments that could be morning sickness.

They decided to wait a couple more weeks just to make sure, and then go to the doctor before announcing it to everybody. Then they could force their parents to sign the consent forms and get married.

One Wednesday after school, about a week before Tina's doctor appointment, Michael headed toward Boggy Creek, which was a few miles east of Enid off Highway 412.

Tina was helping her mom do the grocery shopping that

afternoon. She was trying to be a submissive daughter so her parents wouldn't suspect anything, although Michael wondered if her sudden acquiescence wouldn't be more suspicious than her usual rebellion.

Boggy Creek was mostly wide and shallow as it wound through Northern Oklahoma. It was aptly named, since at some points it was more swamp than creek, with the water spreading out into shallow pools that grew green slime. In the summer those parts smelled pretty rank; in the winter, though, it wasn't so bad.

Michael didn't know who the property belonged to; the fields and woods around the creek were undeveloped. A dirt road – a lease road – led north off the highway toward an oil well, and the rutted track toward the creek branched from it about a quarter mile from the highway.

The spot Michael liked best was about half a mile from the highway. The water there was deeper and moved swiftly enough to keep from stinking, but slowly enough to provide good fishing. It had a rocky spit of land jutting into it which was a perfect place for campfires, and on the other side was a bank about eight feet high with trees growing almost to the edge of it. Their roots jutted out of the mud like snakes frozen in the act of writhing.

It wasn't a secret spot; plenty of people had lit campfires here and had a few beers or cigarettes or both, leaving the trash embedded in the mud or scattered into the tall grass. He and his friends had come out lots of times to fish or shoot at snakes with beebee guns. During warmer weather, he and Tina had occasionally come out and had sex on a blanket up among the trees where they were hidden from the road.

There was no one there that day, though – probably because of the cold front that was turning the edges of the water to an icy crust. February was the worst month of the year for cold, gray dampness.

He broke up a few sticks and piled them around a couple of scrawny logs, wedged a piece of newspaper in between, and lit it with his lighter. The high bank and the trees sheltered him from the worst of the wind, and it didn't take long for the dry wood to catch.

He huddled over the fire for nearly an hour before it was time to either go home or find some more wood. Even though his thinking had mostly gone in excited circles, thinking of his coming wedding and subsequent independence, he'd enjoyed the quiet and wasn't ready to go home yet.

His older sister Susan was split up with her husband Bruce again, so she and the kids had moved in temporarily. They were there all the time even when Susan and Bruce were together, but it was different when they brought their clothes and toys and spent a few nights. They seemed to expand and take over the entire house.

He had gathered a couple of longer branches to break up for the fire when he heard a car pulling off the highway. The creek bank was lower than the field of grass between him and the highway, so he couldn't see the car or the person approaching. He stood on his toes and peered over the grass to see who was coming, hoping it was someone who had cigarettes they didn't mind sharing.

It was his dad getting out of his Pontiac Fury, pulling his thin jean jacket close and shoving his hands into his pockets against the cold as he headed toward Michael. Michael was surprised and a little bit pleased. He didn't see his dad away from the house and everyone else very often.

His dad was the type that only had space in his attention for one person at a time. At home that person was always either Susan or her daughter Jeannie. Unless Michael's mom insisted on having everyone's attention by starting fights and throwing things.

"Hey, Dad," Michael said, stepping up the bank to meet him. "What're you doing here?"

His dad gave him a half grin. "Saw your car from the highway. Thought I'd see what you were up to."

"Just hangin' out," Michael said, as they walked back over to the fire. "Can I bum a cigarette?"

His dad pulled the pack of Camels out of his shirt pocket and tossed them to Michael, and then grabbed the long sticks Michael had found and cracked them over his knee for the fire.

"Thanks," Michael said, lighting the cigarette and taking a drag on it.

"You here by yourself? Where's Tina?" his dad asked, once he'd gotten the fire stirred up again.

"She's doing something with her mom today."

"It's kind of strange to see you without her lately."

Michael nodded. He'd seldom been without a girlfriend since fourth grade, but he'd never had the same one for so long, and never one he could bring around his family. Tina accepted him for who he was, though. She didn't act weird when his parents started fighting, or comment on how dirty the house was, even though her home was the complete opposite. Her mom obeyed her dad in everything, and their house was spotless.

And while Michael's family didn't exactly welcome Tina with open arms, they didn't make fun of her.

"It's kind of cold to be out here, don't you think?" his dad prompted, when he didn't say anything else.

"It's so crazy at the house right now," he said. "I just needed a break."

His dad nodded and lit another cigarette. "Ain't it the truth," he said out of the side of his mouth.

They stood in silence, smoking, until his dad cleared his throat. "Michael, I need to tell you something," he said, looking out toward the sky past the trees on the other bank.

Michael's stomach suddenly felt hard, like it was lined with lead. His dad never talked to him like that, and it didn't sound good.

"The thing is," he continued, gazing off into the sky past the trees on the other bank, "I was thinking as soon as you finished high school, I'd probably leave your mom."

Michael relaxed. "That's cool," he said. "I know you guys aren't happy." He considered mentioning his plan to move out soon. Maybe his dad would like it. It would be exciting to have a little support. "You don't have to wait 'til I graduate," he said.

His dad shook his head. "It's nice you're okay with it, but that's not it," he said. "It's not going to work." He threw his cigarette butt down and ground it out with the toe of his boot. "Your mom's pregnant."

Michael choked on the smoke he was inhaling. He coughed so hard he had to sit down on the muddy rocks of the bank. "Shit," he said, when he could breathe again.

"I know." His dad nodded and pressed his lips together, scowling fiercely.

"Isn't Mom too old?" he asked, trying to think of how old she was.

His dad shook his head. "She's only thirty-eight."

"Oh." Thirty-eight seemed too old to have kids. After all, she had two grandkids. So this baby would be an aunt or an uncle as soon as it was born. And it would be close to the same age as his baby if it turned out Tina was already pregnant, too. Maybe they'd go to school together.

He shook his head. It was too weird. How could his mom

Beth Wilson/Personal Loans

be having a baby? He was the baby, and they hadn't even wanted him.

But maybe it wasn't his dad's baby. It wasn't a secret his mom had plenty of boyfriends through the years. He didn't know of any in the past three or four years, but maybe she'd just done a better job of hiding her relationships. "Are you sure it's yours?" he asked.

His dad gave him a sideways look, hesitated, and then nodded. "Pretty sure. Yeah. It's mine."

Michael sighed. "So you're staying?"

His dad looked so sad Michael thought he might cry. "I'm staying."

Michael tried to imagine what this meant, but he couldn't get his head around it. It was a lot easier to imagine his parents splitting up. He'd hidden in his room while they screamed and beat each other for as long as he could remember, wishing they would either get a divorce or kill each other. "You don't have to stay," he urged. "You could still leave."

His dad raised one eyebrow.

"I wouldn't stay," Michael said. "If it was me."

"You saying, if Tina was having your baby, you'd let her take off with it? You'd be okay with not knowing what was happening with your kid?"

Michael hadn't thought of it that way before. He hadn't really thought about what it meant to have a kid. He'd only thought as far as moving into his own place with Tina. In his daydreams of the past few days, Tina sometimes had a big round belly as she cooked him dinner or did his laundry, but he hadn't thought about what it would be like when they had the baby.

What if Tina did leave him and take his kid? Just because they'd been together a while didn't mean they'd be together forever. She could leave him and take his kid, and he'd never see it. He rubbed his chest, feeling short of breath. She wouldn't do that, would she?

He wanted to think he could trust her, but deep down he knew they were both just kids, and who knew what would happen.

His dad stared at him. "What's wrong?"

Michael shook his head, still feeling short of breath. "I just never thought of it that way before."

"Well, you got a while before you have to worry about it," his dad said, lighting another cigarette.

He realized it was probably better to let his dad think that.

This conversation wasn't about him, really, and he was better off leaving it alone.

The thing was, even though he knew it was dumb, he wanted to tell his dad he was having a kid, too. He wanted his dad to keep talking to him as an equal.

"I think you're right," Michael said, standing up and dusting off the seat of his pants. "I wouldn't be able to leave my kid, either."

His dad grunted and looked out past the trees on the opposite bank, studying the sky. Michael had already lost him.

"Tina might be pregnant," Michael blurted out. "We figured we'd wait a couple more weeks 'til we knew for sure, and then we'd get married."

His dad turned sharply toward him, scowling, and slapped him across the side of his head, nearly knocking him over. "You dumb shit! What were you thinking?"

"Ow!" Michael gingerly put his hand over his cheek and ear, surprised when he didn't find blood. His ear felt like it had been torn loose of his head. "You and Mom did the same thing," he said defensively.

"That's how I know it's stupid." His dad threw his hands in the air in frustration. He sounded completely disgusted. "If you learned anything from me, it should've been to not have kids. Kids are nothing but trouble. Have you not seen how miserable my whole fucking life has been?"

Michael felt confused. One second his dad loved his kids so much he couldn't leave his abusive relationship, and the next he hated his kids for ruining his life. Was he supposed to feel loved or guilty?

"I never knew you stayed for us," Michael mumbled.

"Why else would I stay?" He picked up a fist-sized rock and hurled it at the roots on the other side, knocking a chunk out of one. Its white insides looked raw and wet. "Why the fuck would I stay?"

"I'm sorry I was born!" Michael said, raising his voice, but careful not to actually yell. He didn't want to get his other ear slapped. "I just wish Mom had had an abortion instead of having me so you could leave her and be happy and not have a miserable fucking life."

His dad stared at him for a few long seconds, frowning.

Then he sighed and pulled out the cigarettes again. He

handed one to Michael as a conciliatory gesture. Michael thought about refusing, but that would end the conversation for sure. As long as he stayed there was a chance things could get better.

He took the cigarette and leaned in so his dad *could* light it for him, and they squatted in front of the fire and smoked in silence, staring at the tangled roots and feeling miserable together. The last of the fire fell in on itself and died.

"You got a plan, then?" his dad said, after he stubbed out his cigarette butt.

"Yeah. We're getting married," Michael said.

"No, I mean a plan," his dad said. "Where will you live? How will you support a kid? What about school?"

"I have a job," he said. "I'm working on the rest. Maybe I'll just quit school and get my G.E.D. so I can work full time."

His dad sighed and shook his head. "At least Robbie's going to graduate."

"Maybe the new one will graduate, too," Michael said bitterly. "Then you'll have two good ones."

His dad looked over at him. "School don't make you good or bad," he said. "I just wanted things to be easier for you."

"If you wanted things to be easier for me, you should have moved out and took me with you," Michael said harshly. "You shouldn't have made me stay there while you guys beat the shit out of each other."

His dad sighed and rubbed his temples with the tips of his middle fingers. "Maybe so, Michael. It's hard to say. It ain't easy to change your whole life, not knowing if the change'll be any better than what you had, or if it'll be a million times worse. It ain't easy to get away from someone you been with your whole fuckin' life."

Michael nodded. His dad had stayed for him, and he'd stayed for himself. They could both be true, he supposed. Besides, Michael didn't like being alone, either. He hugged his knees harder and shivered. This new perspective on his life wasn't pleasant, and he didn't know what to do with it.

The pebbles and rocks he was sitting on had been worn smooth from years of erosion in a creek bed, but they were still biting into his scrawny butt. He felt chilled all the way to his bones. He stood up and shook himself, dusting off the seat of his jeans and then jamming his hands back into his pockets.

"I gotta get back," he said. "I'm freezing."

"Yeah." His dad sighed and stood up, too. He looked around

at the landscape again, and then back at Michael. "Let's keep this between ourselves," he said.

"Right." he agreed.   As if there was anybody he could tell. He felt like his dad had handed him a boulder to carry around on his back.

He started to pick his way across the rocks to the path, and then paused and turned. "So you won't tell Mom about Tina, either?"

His dad frowned. "It'll wait a bit, I suppose. I'll give you the time, but don't expect any support. You're on your own."

Michael nodded. "I never expected anything."   That was true enough.

"I made my own way in this world. You can do the same."

"I know." Michael scowled. "I said I don't need anything. I'm fine."

His dad shrugged his shoulders and turned away.

Michael walked back to his Jeep slowly, hoping that his dad would call him back and say something to cross the gap that was spreading out between them.   He resisted the urge to look over his shoulder, though.

The wind was pretty harsh away from the protection of the creek banks, and it was a relief to climb into the driver's seat.   He pulled the rearview mirror down to study his ear.   It wasn't much redder than the other one.

Before he pulled off the bumpy track onto the highway to go back into town he glanced behind him, but there was still no sign of his dad.

Gerald Locklin

Gerald Locklin is a Professor Emeritus of English at California State University, Long Beach, where he continues teaching as an occasional part-time lecturer there and in the Master of Professional Writing Program at USC. His most recent books are *Gerald Locklin: New and Selected Poems*, World Parade Books, 2008; *The Plot of Il Trovatore*, Kamini Books, 2009; *A Sinatra Sequence*, Zerx Press, 2009; and *The Dodger's Retirement Party: A Novella*, from Aortic Press, 2010. *Selected Recent Stories* is forthcoming in 2010 from World Parade Books. He is also the subject of the 512 page *Gerald Locklin: A Critical Introduction*, edited by Michael Basinski, from BlazeVOX Books, 2010.

See also: www.geraldlocklin.com, www.lummoxpress.com, www.worldparadebooks.net, www.aorticpress.net, www.nyquarterly.com, www.chironreview.com, www.wormwoodreview.com, www.kaminipress.com, The Gerald Locklin Collection is archived at www.csulb/library/specialcollections/locklin

Beth Wilson

Beth was born and raised in Oklahoma. She got a Bachelor's degree in English from the University of Central Oklahoma, and a Library Science degree from the University of Oklahoma. It was while she was studying creative writing at UCO that she met the poet and author Gerald Locklin, and an immediate friendship sprang up that has been maintained over time and half the country mainly by e-mail.

As a full-time reference librarian and mother of two small children, Beth writes short stories and poetry whenever she can find a few minutes strung together. This usually means that she doesn't get much sleep. But, after all, that's what coffee is for.

She uses her own observations and experiences from the "heartland" as well as stories she gathers from her husband and friends to fuel her writing. Her chapbook, *School of Sky*, was nominated for a Pushcart Prize. She prefers to write near a window so she can look outside and see what the weather is doing.

ABOUT LUMMOX PRESS

Lummox Press was created in 1994 by RD Armstrong. It began as a self-publishing/DIY imprint for poetry by RD. Several chapbooks were published and in late 1995 it began publishing the Lummox Journal, a monthly small/underground press lit-arts zine. Available primarily by subscription, the LJ continued its exploration of the "creative process" until its demise as a print mag in 2006.

During its eleven year existence, this tiny mag with the big name, interviewed poets, musicians and artists (over 100 in all) about how they do what they do. Hundreds of poems were also published in its pages. Poets like *Todd Moore, Lyn Lifshin, Gerald Locklin, Holly Prado, L.A. Bogen, Linda Lerner, Scott Wannberg, Philomene Long, John Thomas* and *RD Armstrong,* to name a few, appeared regularly within its pages. It was hailed as one of the best monthlies in the small press.

In 1998, Lummox began publishing the Little Red Book series, and continues to do so today. To date there are some 63 titles in the series (as of 2009) and this year a collection of poems from the first decade of the series has been published under the title, The Long Way Home (2009).

Lummox has published the following titles: The Wren Notebook by Rick Smith (2000); Last Call: The Legacy of Charles Bukowski (2004); Fire and Rain– Selected Poems 1993-2007 Volumes 1 & 2 by RD Armstrong (2008); On/Off the Beaten Path (a trio of long poems about road trips taken in 1999, 2000 and 2001 including the epic poem RoadKill– which John Berbrich said was "the best post 9-11 writing I've seen") by RD Armstrong (2008);

El Pagano and Other Twisted Tales (a collection of short stories and flash fiction) by RD Armstrong (2008); New and Selected Poems by John Yamrus (2008); The Riddle of the Wooden Gun by Todd Moore (2009); Sea Trails by Pris Campbell (2009); Down This Crooked Road– Modern Poetry from the Road Less Traveled edited by RD Armstrong and William Taylor, Jr. (2009); Drive By– Shards & Poems by John Bennett; Modest Aspirations by Gerald Locklin (poems) and Beth Wilson (stories) (2010); and Steel Valley by Michael Adams (2010). These books are available directly from the Lummox Press via the website: www.lummoxpress.com or at Lummox c/o PO Box 5301 San Pedro, CA 90733. There are also E-Book versions of most titles available. You can also buy them via major online sellers...

Together with Chris Yeseta (Layout and Art Direction since 1997), RD continues to publish books that are both striking in their looks as well as their content...

Please visit the website to read selections from these titles as well as peruse the many other titles/articles published by the Lummox Press.

www.ingramcontent.com/pod-product-compliance
Lightning Source LLC
Chambersburg PA
CBHW071127250626

47159CB00006B/2164